MAYBE SHORTY SHOULD BE A DETECTIVE

Copyright 2016

Written by: Heather Jay Harris
Edited by: C.K. Brooke
Cover Art: Tayler Haywood

Everything I do is for Christion. But I also need to thank my real life inspirations: Tehran, Brandon and Jalisa.

Chantay and Woo, I write your names so that I never forget you.

Chapter One

The bang of the gavel crashing against the sound block might have been a sonic boom for the effect it had on Chelsea. She felt light headed, she wanted to faint. She wanted to vomit. Her brother Carter put his arm around her as the officers placed handcuffs on James to escort him out of the courtroom.

"I love you Chelsea!" he screamed while being pulled away. "Don't come see me! Carter! Don't let her come! Take care of the baby!" He was reaching out to her and she was reaching back. She couldn't speak.

"I told you not to date him. Any man in his late twenties still sagging his pants is a waste of time," Carter said. "And now he's a convicted felon."

Chelsea broke away from Carter and walked out of the courtroom. He followed but she walked faster. He called her name and she didn't respond. She simply got into the elevator. He chased her to the closing elevator doors. Their eyes met, his in remorse, hers in anger.

"I'm sorry Chels," he offered softly.

She dropped her head. Carter was the police officer that had arrested James.

"I know," she replied, tears streaming from her eyes.

The elevator doors opened on the first floor to the waiting reporters and their aggressive camera flashes. It was all Chelsea could do to hold in her tears, her rage, and her vomit. The morning sickness had been especially rough the last few days. She moved through the journalists with only a "No comment" barely audible. She glanced over at James's mother and sister standing against a wall. Guess they weren't as interesting as the future baby momma of the convict who just happened to be the younger sister of the arresting officer. James's sister Denise wrapped her arm around Chelsea and pushed her way through the revolving doors of the Wayne County Courthouse.

"Are you okay Chelsea?" Denise asked.

"No comment." Chelsea answered again.

"Do you need me to take you home?"

"No. I can call a Lyft."

"Stop trippin'. I'm driving you," Denise demanded.

"No," Chelsea said, pulling away.

"Why not?"

"Because Carter is still my brother. I won't listen to you say anything bad about him. And in your shoes, what else would you say? Chelsea's voice quivered. "I just want to be alone. I'll be fine."

Chelsea walked down the street. She reached the corner, turned and looked up at the edifice of so-called justice that would house James for another day before shipping him off to the Dickerson Correctional Facility. Then she looked down at the budding green grass of spring and threw up until she gagged.

Chapter Two

DeMykel's Chevy Trailblazer pulled up to the corner of Congress and Randolph in downtown Detroit just a block from the courthouse. Chelsea's phone chimed alerting her to his arrival. He jumped out the car and ran to open the rear passenger door.

"My queen." he said.

Chelsea got in and was immediately nauseated by the smell of lavender incense burning. He was one of those guys. The kind that burned incense in a car.

"I am DeMykel, your driver for this fine afternoon. It is my pleasure to be your chariot. May I offer you a pH balanced bottle of water?"

"Why does your car smell like a healing ritual gone wrong? The dollar store has perfectly good air fresheners," Chelsea said letting her window down.

"How about a cookie or brownie?" he said. "My sister makes them. They're really good."

"Edibles? No thank you. I'm pregnant," Chelsea replied.

"Who said they were edibles?" DeMykel asked, smiling at her through the rear view mirror.

"You just seem the type to sling a little green out the Lyft on the side. I have a sixth sense about these kinds of things." And she did.

"I have regular cookies too. My sister is an amazing cook. I'm only driving to help save money for her restaurant.She studied at the Culinary Institute in Rochester Hills. That's the best cooking school in the Midwest. If you're interested in donating to her GoFundMe page, I have a flyer with more information. Black people need to stick together like the Arabs and the Jews do. Keep our money in our own community." He was also the type to lecture a stranger in the Lyft, and then ask for money.

"How long has she been cooking?"

"About fifteen years.She started right out of high school. And I mean, that girl can burn! Her macaroni and cheese..."

Chelsea cut him off mid-sentence. "But the Institute relocated to Chicago on April 29,1996. I remember reading it in the paper."

DeMykel looked at her again through the rear view. "When did you read that?"

"I just told you. April 29, 1996."

"Like you got that kind of recall." His tone was incredulous. "How old was you? Ten?"

"I was seven." Chelsea bit her lip. "Sorry. Today has been crazy. I'm sure your sister is a great cook. And I hope she gets her restaurant. But, then again, you don't have to lie to make her seem better. It doesn't matter how she got good at cooking. Some people go to fancy schools, some had grannies who taught them. But lying for money is low key fraud. Right? I want to support a black business, not a black lie. You feel me, Boo?"

DeMykel nodded. He didn't say much for the rest of the ride. When he dropped her off on Plymouth Road, he asked, "Can you wait a minute?" He pulled out his phone and began to clack at the screen. Chelsea knew he was googling the Institute in hopes of proving her wrong. After a few seconds his eyes got big. "Detroit Free Press. April 29, 1996. Culinary Institute Relocates to Windy City." He looked at her in amazement. "Are you anointed by God? Like a prophet?"

Chelsea snickered. "Prophets can see the future. I just remember stuff I read. Stop being dramatic." She exited his vehicle and made a mental note to give him one star in her review.

Chapter Three

She didn't live on Plymouth Road. She just asked to be dropped off there. It was the main street for the Elmirdale community and where all the stores were. The day had already been too much stress, too much incense and too much nausea. A short walk in the fresh air would do her good and maybe settle her stomach. If not, she'd grab a ginger ale from Sam's Party Store on her way home.

"Hey Shorty." Big T waived at Chelsea as she walked past his house. "Yo booty gettin' big. What you been eating?" Chelsea winced at the sound of his voice. He had been salivating over her body since they were thirteen and she first got her curves. Always to her annoyance. "I'm pregnant Theodrick."

"You out here calling people by their government names? Really Chelsea?" He put extra emphasis on her name. It didn't have nearly the same impact. "Who yo baby daddy? James?"

She stopped in her step and glared up at him.

"Heard he murked one of the Fontaines on Joy Road. Is that true?" Big T asked.

"Of course not. But when has that ever stopped a black man from going to jail?"

"I know that's right. It's prolly for the best though. Them Fontaines is some crazy Creoles. He might be safer in lock up."

Chelsea shrugged. He gave her body the full up and down with his eyes. "But you shouldn't be by yourself right now. Let me keep you company."

Chelsea couldn't hold it in. Another vomit. Right on his lawn. She wiped her mouth.

"There yo answer." She walked away.

"That was cold. Chels! Real cold! I thought we was better than that!" he hollered behind her. She smiled. First time all day.

She continued to make her way down the block, just minutes away from her house. Her phone chimed again. This time a call from her father Ray, no doubt at Carter's request. Not even Daddy could broker a peace treaty between siblings today.

Chelsea knew she would eventually make her peace with Carter. He was only doing his job. And all the evidence did point to James. But there was a huge part of her, the emotional part, possibly the hormonal part too that just expected Carter to trust her. To trust James. He knew him. They had spent a lot of time together over the past year while he dated Chelsea. Why couldn't Carter see that James was framed? Why couldn't

Carter ever see what was right in front of his face? Sometimes he was too much cop for his own good.

Today was a day when Chelsea could neither deal with her father nor her big brother. She needed her mom. Diane French was the only person that ever really understood her daughter. Probably because they were so much alike. When teachers would refer to Chelsea as problematic and different, Diane would just hug her. "You are very special baby girl. You just need to learn how to use that mind of yours for something good," she would say to Chelsea, usually after leaving the principal's office on one of her bad behavior days.

Chelsea decided to ignore Ray's phone call. "If only Ma was here. She'd tell me what to do."

She reached the front stoop of the house that she was born and raised in. The house where her parents had once loved each other. After Diane's death Ray quickly remarried and moved away leaving Chelsea the house. Now she lived alone since Detective Carter French thought he was too affluent to live in Elmirdale anymore. To hear him tell it, he had outgrown the old neighborhood.

Chelsea expected to never outgrow it. It was home.

"Carter called me. He's worried about you," her next-door neighbor, Snap, said, walking off his porch and approaching her.

"Worried about me? I'm worried about Car. He forgot where he came from."

Snap extended one of his well-toned arms around her shoulders. Her head fell onto his chest.

"Pretty bad day, huh?"

Chelsea nodded. "Theodrick said it was for the best. At least the Fontaines can't get to him if he's in Dickerson."

"What does Theodrick know? He was still blowing chocolate milk out of his nose in high school. Did you eat today?"

"Yeah. I left half of it on the courthouse lawn and the other half down the street with Theodrick."

He patted her shoulder sympathetically. "Well, you probably need to brush your teeth now. Let's go inside."

He followed Chelsea up the five stairs that led to her front door. She fumbled in her purse to find her keys. "My Lyft driver was selling weed cookies and promoting a GoFundMe. You better get yo cousin." She unlocked the door and they walked inside.

"You know how we do it in the D, Chels. We like it nice and grimy."

Snap closed the door behind him.

Chapter Four

At about seven-fifteen on a Wednesday evening, Carter gently rapped on the screen door to the house he was born and raised in. Normally, he would just walk in without announcing his arrival. but Chels had been so weird the last month that he didn't want to upset her. When he'd called and asked if he could come over, he wasn't even sure if she'd say it was all right.
She opened the door for him and he walked in, put a six-pack of Corona on the coffee table and crashed in their father's old easy chair. He pulled a half-eaten bag of pretzels out of his pocket, grabbed a beer, and exhaled. It was a very comfortable chair.

"I shoulda held out for Dad's chair. Fought you for it. Custody battle."

"Just try it. That chair ain't leaving this house. But, since it's technically half-yours, you are welcome to come over and sit in it whenever you like."

Carter laughed. "I hate the ghetto too much for that. I don't understand how you can live here."

"It's amazing the things that you'll say while accepting the hospitality of my ghetto digs."

"But you know I'm right. You shouldn't still be living here."

"If I ain't tripping, why are you?"

"Ain't?" he asked.

"You came over to give me an English lesson?"

After high school Carter had completed two years of junior college before he was accepted into the police academy. He preferred a poorly lit one-bedroom apartment on the third floor of an overpriced suburban apartment building to the complimentary room and board in the dwelling his father had left him and his sister before moving to Florida with his wealthy second wife. After a couple of years in blue he upgraded to a pretty plush condominium off of some lake in Oakland County. Their father's rich second wife had generously provided the down-payment money (as penance for being in the picture before their mother had died). She'd bought Chelsea a car, previously owned.

Carter loved serving the city of Detroit. He just didn't want to live there. And it only took him eight years to become a detective. Homicide. But it's Detroit. Everything is homicide.

"I'm just saying, you can remember a quote you read about President Obama two years ago, but can't remember to say isn't instead of ain't.

"I remember. I just don't care." That was always Chelsea's response to Carter's grammar corrections. "Besides, I isn't trippin is also incorrect."

He smiled as he cracked open his first brew. The fatigue of the day washed off his face as he guzzled it straight down. He sat up and grabbed another and offered her one.

"You know I can't," she declined.

"Oh that's right, off the sauce for six more months. I really did mean to take you to the doctor the other day, but you didn't call me."

"It's okay. The first few months are routine. It's just heartbeats. It doesn't get good till the ultrasound."

"So how's James?" he asked. As soon as he said it, he knew he messed up. Carter had a way of ruining a good flow. Why did he have to mention the very subject that caused their last month of tension?

"That's a silly question. He was found guilty. He's in jail for eight to fifteen. You were there, you heard the verdict. How do you think he is?"

"I didn't come over here to fight with you about James again. But you can't still believe he's innocent?"

Chelsea decided to walk into the kitchen and take a few seconds before answering. This was their first time talking since that day. He watched her take a deep breath before returning to the living room.

Before she could respond, Carter interjected, "Let's not talk about that. How are things at the grocery mart?"

"Is this what I have to look forward to tonight, Carter? First it's the neighborhood, then it's my grammar, then James, and now it's my job! I don't work at the grocery mart. I work at Farmer Roger's, a reputable and well-established chain that has been in business for many years. I'm in a union, I have an IRA, life insurance and medical benefits. I make more money than some cops. You know what else? I don't pay rent, so I have a nice, healthy bank account. Can you get off my back, please?"

Farmer Roger's was where Chelsea had been hired after high school.

Maybe Carter was being too patronizing. "Chelsea, I just think you're selling yourself short."
He'd barely been in the house five minutes, and he had already made her angry. She stormed into the kitchen and opened the refrigerator.

"How do I work at a grocery store and have an empty refrigerator?" she scolded herself.

14

She took two oranges out and walked back into the living room. Carter was now on his fourth beer and her phone was ringing. She glanced at the screen before answering. It was Snap.

"Hey, Snap. Carter's here. I'll call you back when he leaves. Bye." She hung up.

"I'm glad to see Snap is holding up his end of the deal and looking out for you." Carter laughed. He went to grab another beer. Chelsea reached over and took the remaining two.

"I think you're done, Detective French. You still have to drive all the way back to Something-Something Township. Unless you want to crash here tonight. Heaven help us." She put the two beers in the refrigerator, promising herself she wouldn't have one sip.

"Novi Township. And you're right, I'm not staying here. So, what you got up for the night?" Carter said desperately trying to make small talk.

"Snap's cable is out. He's trying to come over to watch television." Chelsea had begun to peel her orange.

Carter decided it was time to tell her the other reason for his visit.

"There was a murder today. A man was stabbed at a fruit stand in Eastern Market." His face was solemn as he pulled out a small black notepad.

"Is that why you're here, Car? Don't detectives have to pass some kind of exam? Aren't you supposed to have your own powers of deduction? I'm no cop." This was not the first time Carter had called upon his baby sister's help on a case. He had even taken her on a stakeout once. She wasn't allowed out of the car.

As children, Carter had noticed that Chelsea had an uncanny gift. She remembered every word uttered within earshot. She could always tell when someone was lying and when even the smallest item was out of place. When Michael Simpson had stolen Carter's bike when he was thirteen, it was an eleven-year-old Chelsea who'd trapped him in his lies and made him return it. But it wasn't until they were much older that Carter realized how valuable she could be to him.

Chapter Five

A week before James's conviction, Carter's promotion to detective had become official. It was his work on the Fontaine case that had earned him the promotion. At that point James was in a holding cell but had yet to be sentenced. And even though he and Chelsea were constantly arguing over the case, she was still optimistic enough in the justice system to be happy for Carter. Their father and his second wife had flown into town to celebrate Carter's promotion. News of Chelsea's pregnancy had just hit the fan, so Carter knew the reason for their visit had layers.

Their first night in town, Ray French had taken his family to dinner at a popular restaurant in Something-Something Township. Carter sat across from the old boy who ordered a bottle of the finest champagne. Chelsea had sat at his left, and his rich wife on his right.

Carter liked his father's new wife. And not just because she had given him the money for his condo. He genuinely found her to be a fascinating woman. She'd won the state lottery and was worth millions. But prior to that, she worked with Chelsea at Farmer Roger's. She'd been the manager. Her conversation ranged anywhere from her cousin Dwayne shooting dice on the corner to where to find the best crepes in Paris.

Chelsea, on the other hand, considered an allegiance with this woman a betrayal to her dead mother. Ever since winning the lottery and becoming a woman of wealth and leisure, her ex-manager had insisted everyone call her Miss Madeleine, but Chelsea still called her Maddy just to annoy her. And Chelsea did very little to hide her dislike.

For the night though, Chelsea would muster up enough politeness to avoid her father's reproach.

"How are you baby?" Ray French had asked, leaning across the table to hold his daughter's hand.

"I'm fine." Chelsea hoped she wouldn't be the only topic of conversation for the evening.

"What's fine about being pregnant by a man in jail and living all alone?" Miss Madeleine had scoffed. "You ain't the first girl to get knocked up by a convict. I could tell a story or two, but this ain't the time or the place. It's Carter's night."

Actually, everyone had been eager that night to hear the details of Carter's first week as a real detective. He was already working on an important case. One of the mayor's bodyguards had been shot leaving a movie theater with his wife. On the surface, it appeared to be a random carjacking. His wife described the assailant, and disclosed in great detail how they were attacked in the parking lot, their car stolen, and her husband shot at close range. Two days later, Carter's partner uncovered a brewing scandal involving the mayor and some secrets no one had wanted to get out.

By the time Carter sat to break bread with his family, it was the consensus of the bosses upstairs that the bodyguard was shot because he was going to blow the whistle on something...or someone.

He'd read from his little black notepad the wife's description of the assailant. He was white, tall, over six foot, with chestnut brown hair. He wore a baseball cap pulled down over his face so the bodyguard's wife couldn't see his eyes. But she was sure if she ever heard his voice again, she'd recognize it. The department figured this to be some kind of professional hit. They were using their underground connections to find the guy. They located the car, a 2012 BMW 545i. There were too many different sets of prints.

They had identified the victim's, the wife's, and several family members. They could only hope that one of the other sets belonged to the hit man, although that was unlikely. Between that and the wife's identification, hopefully they'd have enough to put him away once they found him. If they found him.

Carter had sat back that evening and looked at his family. He could see the pride in his father's eyes. Even Chelsea was beaming. Miss Madeleine looked perplexed. Carter could understand how the details of a police investigation might confuse a woman like her.

"So, Chelsea, I guess you keeping this baby," She said.

"I didn't want to bring it up but since it's on the table... How are you going to manage Chelsea?" Ray French had diverted all of his attention to his youngest child.

Chelsea cleared her throat. "What movie theater, Carter?"

The Bel-Air on the east side," he said as once again it was The Chelsea Show.

"James and I went there once. I remember being nervous walking to the car. The parking lot was too dark," she replied.

"That makes it a perfect place for a hit." Ray French passed the bread to his wife who had already had four pieces.

"Were there any cars in the lot not accounted for? He left in their car so how'd he get there?" Chelsea was desperately trying to keep the subject off of her own drama. "What time did the movie let out? Did they have another car?"

"I don't understand why you're asking all these questions," Miss Madeleine had said. "Carter has already solved the case. You need to be asking yourself how you're going to support that baby!"

Carter had ignored Miss Madeleine but appreciated the faith she had in him. It was obvious to him what Chelsea was doing. He decided to play along if for no other reason than to enjoy the extra attention he was getting, "The movie let out at nine-fifteen and the Beamer was the wife's car. His car was a Cadillac Deville. Where are you going with all this, Chels?"

"You have to figure that whoever killed this guy knew he would be at the movies with his wife that night." Chelsea was now directing the entire conversation toward Carter.

"At least tell me that this James dude had a savings account. Something put up for a rainy day or jail sentence," Ray French chimed in between bites of pasta.

Carter decided to join Chelsea in ignoring the parent group. "It was date night. They went every Wednesday at seven. Anyone could have found that out."

"Think about it Car, bodyguards are fighters. They're trained not to let folks get too close. You said there was no sign of a struggle and yet this guy gets shot at close range? It had to be someone he already knew." She was talking fast.

"Ray, I think Chelsea should come live with us, at least until she has the baby," Miss Madeleine had said decisively.

At that point all conversation ceased. Chelsea's mouth had dropped open and Carter's mind was filled with images of wig hairs in the bathroom sink and pig feet for breakfast.

"In the guest house, of course. You'd have your own space. We wouldn't bother you," Miss Madeleine continued.

"Carter!" Chelsea had yelled out not realizing how loud she was. She took a breath and in a much softer tone said, "Was he a big guy? Why would he want to ride in that baby Beamer when he could be in his big Cadillac?"

Most inhabitants of the Motor City fluently spoke and understood the auto language. From the rich to the poor, practically every Detroiter knew far too much about cars. "Yeah, he was pretty big. Who knows why she drove? Maybe he was tired, or maybe she doesn't like his driving. Does it really matter, Chels?"

"I worked at Farmer Roger's. I know how bad the health plan is. Whatever doctor you seeing is probably some Indian quack. But if you come down to Florida you'll have your baby at the best hospital in Boca with a private room and a Jewish doctor. Nothing but the best for our daughter."

Carter braced for a reaction. Between the blatantly racist remark about her Punjabi obstetrician, and the expression 'our daughter', he expected Chelsea would blow her stack.

"I like Dr. Punta-Shah!" Chelsea's hand hit the table. Then, redirecting back to Carter she'd said, "But if you can't tell me how he got there, I'm not buying this whole professional hit man angle. What did he do? Take the bus? A cab?"

"Dad, I'm going to help Chels with the baby. I'll take her to the doctor and all that stuff. She can even come stay with me if

22

she wants." Carter gave Chelsea a sly wink before his next comment to her. "Did it ever occur to you that the killer might have parked his car somewhere other than the movie theater parking lot?"

"Where? There's nothing else over there but a gas station and a few houses. If that was the case, someone should have seen the car parked. Did you ask around the neighborhood?"

Of course the police had canvassed the neighborhood, looking for witnesses or anything else out of place. The Detroit Police Department certainly did not need Chelsea French, cashier, to tell them basic operating procedures. But Carter decided to humor her. "Yes, we did, Inspector, and no one saw anything."

"I think you two need to hear Miss Madeleine out. She's making a good point. Chelsea, you can't stay in that neighborhood all by yourself. I may need to make an executive decision," Ray French touted.

Usually an easygoing man, it wasn't often that Ray French made an executive decision for the family. But when he did, nothing less than the hand of God could dissuade him. Ray had once decided that his money would not be spent on overpriced designer sneakers for his teenage children—in fact, they couldn't cost more than thirty dollars. This particular executive decision had made Carter the laughing stock of the boys' locker room and earned him the nickname 'Slips'.

Chelsea dropped her glass in despair as Carter jumped in to save her.

"Dad, no. I mean...why not give her some time? She's barely eight weeks along. We don't need to make all these decisions right now. I'm sure she has a plan." He laughed nervously, not sure if Ray would let go so easily. Ray and Miss Madeleine turned toward Chelsea, who was bending over to pick up the glass. Carter was wrong, she didn't have a plan.

"I'll marry Snap," she said before she could stop herself. Miss Madeleine made a horrible gasp while Ray French calmly shook his head.

"When did he ask you?" Ray questioned.

"He's been asking me since seventh grade." Chelsea laughed and silently thanked the line manager at the General Motors Stamping plant for having given Snap overtime that night. Or else he would have certainly tagged along.

"I thought Snap was just your friend?" Miss Madeleine cut in. "Now, my friends will do anything for me. But they ain't gon' marry me."

"I married you. I'm your friend. You don't need no more friends." Ray said.

"Snap is my very b-best friend," Chelsea stammered, "and that's what everyone wants, right? To marry their best friend?"

"Well, I never thought I'd hear myself say marrying Snap was a good idea. That boy don't do nothing but wash his car and buy gym shoes. But it's your best option." Ray French beckoned for the waitress.

Just as Chelsea had heaved a sigh of relief, Miss Madeleine exclaimed with annoyance, "Whose baby is it really, Chelsea? Is it Snap's? You might as well tell us! The baby gon' probably come out looking just like him. Then what you gon' do?"

The waitress made her way over to the table. As she leaned over to take Ray's plate Chelsea caught a glimpse of her hair under the light. It was brown, but when she stood, it looked black. "Excuse me, I don't mean to sound rude, but what color is your hair?" Chelsea inquired of the waitress. Anything to deflect from the excruciating turn this conversation with her family had taken.

"I know...everyone thinks its black, but it's actually brown. I just got it dyed last week. They call the color Deep," the waitress replied with a smile before taking dessert orders.

Everyone thinks it's black.

"Chelsea! You know you can tell us the truth! Does the baby belong to the thug in jail or the little boy next door?" Miss Madeleine asked defiantly. But Chelsea wasn't listening anymore. She was staring at Carter with her head tilted to the side and her face scrunched up.

"Chelsea! What's the matter with you?" he asked.

"I think his wife killed him."

"The wife is not the killer Chelsea! Don't you think trained professionals like us would have already checked her story? The other witnesses that saw them being carjacked reported seeing the wife with her hands up, screaming. They just weren't close enough to identify the killer. This man died because he knew too much," Carter said, raising his voice. He didn't mind helping her deal with the folks, but he wasn't about to let her make a fool of him or the Detroit Police Department.

"Ray French! You'd better not let this girl marry that Snap until she know who her baby daddy is! You are still the head of this family and you need to do something for your daughter!" Miss Madeleine cried out refusing to drop the subject. Chelsea and Carter were getting a sample of the determined resilience that could lure a married man away from his wife and children.

"Why do you think it's the wife, baby?" Ray asked her.

Carter went to interrupt but Ray motioned for him to be quiet.

"The hair. She said the killer had chestnut brown hair. She couldn't have seen that at night. She would've said black or even dark hair, but not brown. She's lying." Chelsea finished her glass of water, wishing it was a shot of Tequila. "The real killer is probably short, black and bald."

Carter wanted to be mad, but he couldn't be. His baby sister was making a lot of sense. He sighed heavily. "What do you think happened?"

"She hired someone to kill her husband. Someone he knew. Maybe a relative or a friend. Could be why she insisted on driving her car that night. Could be your killer really did catch the bus because he's probably an amateur. The husband must have told her what was going on at work. She knew if anything happened, you guys would uncover something shady and blame it on that."

"Why did she insist on driving?" Ray asked.

"I don't know but I'm pretty sure she needed to be the driver in control for the plan to work. What if the movie let out before her hitman got there? She needed to stall for time. You know, pretend she left something or circle the lot. Ask her when you talk to her, Carter."

"Hey Dad, she's still got it," Carter said with a smirk.

"Yes, she does," Ray French said with pride, taking Chelsea's hand. "I think you got yourself a secret weapon, Son."

"You figured all that out just from Carter's little story?" Miss Madeleine's face was perplexed. Chelsea just ignored her and jammed a fork into a giant piece of chocolate cheesecake.

Carter spent the majority of the ride home on the phone with his captain and his partner, explaining Chelsea's alternate theory of the crime—taking full credit, of course. The Captain agreed that it was time to have a different conversation with the wife. After hanging up, Carter looked over at her in the passenger seat. She had a sleepy face and was seconds from dozing off.

"You gonna tell Snap you're getting married?" he snickered.

"Of course. He won't mind. He'll have my back if it will keep me in Detroit. He is my best friend. But in seven months when I call off our engagement and Dad tries to kill him, that's when he may be a little pissed."

Carter laughed.

Chapter Six

In the Monday morning edition of the Detroit Free Press, there was a picture of Carter and the mayor with a caption that read: "After only one week on the job, Detective Carter French, 29, solves bodyguard homicide."

As it turned out, the bodyguard's wife had found a new love. Fearful of her husband's wrath when she attempted to leave him, she decided to dissolve their marriage in a more biblical way... till death. She enlisted the help of her hapless brother who was positively identified by a taxi driver as the nervous man he'd dropped at the movie theater.

The mayor, never a man to miss a photo opportunity, was so pleased to have the case solved before his dirty laundry hit the press, that he personally gave Carter his very first commendation.

He'd also received a bonus. Half he'd spent on himself at Neiman Marcus, the other half was set aside for Chelsea's baby.

No one in the department knew it was Carter's baby sister, the bicycle finder, who'd actually solved the case. And as he now sat in her living room, drinking beer after beer, he needed her again.

"Detectives need facts and intuition. I'm all out of both. You have to help me." He begged.

"Why don't you just frame somebody? Isn't that what police do?" Chelsea's tone was malicious.

"Chelsea, this isn't about James. It's about Erik Peterson. A man who went to buy some fruit on his lunch break and ended up dead."

This had been his first request for her help since James was convicted.

"Yes, it is about James! You didn't listen to me when I told you he was innocent. But now you want me to help you with somebody I don't care about?"

"James is guilty. You need to face that and stop blaming me! There were three of us on that case. I was the junior of the team. My superiors sent me to arrest him and I did my job! My job, Chels!" he screamed.

"Stop yelling at me! I'm not helping you, and that's that! If it's your job, then you need to do it. And get it right this time!"

Carter's face was turning red. Ray and Diane would have separated the siblings by now. But without them there, the daggers were sure to come out.

"What's that supposed to mean?

"It means of your last two murder cases, you got one wrong, and the other I had to do for you!"

"Are you saying I can't do my job?"

"I'm saying, for the sake of the Petersons, try not to arrest the wrong man."

Carter didn't say a word. He just stormed out the house. She had hurt him. But he had hurt her too.

The French siblings were at odds now. The last time that happened, Carter was in college, angry with Chelsea for taking his car without asking. They didn't speak for three days, and Ray French had threatened to beat them with a switch if they didn't make up.

Ray French might not have been able to find a switch big enough this time.

Chapter Seven

Chelsea and her teenage second cousin, Olive, sat on the porch of the house Chelsea's father left his children before moving to Boca Raton with his second wife, Miss Madeleine. Chelsea's brother, Carter, quite snobbishly declined his half of the house in favor of more affluent surroundings in Oakland County. But Chelsea was a D-girl to the bone. She refused to move out of Detroit.

"That's what the white man wants us to do," Chelsea would say. "Then he moves back and takes the city away from us." To which Carter would always reply, "He can have it. It's a sewer."

But on this afternoon, there was no looming gloom of Carter's elitist voice. The sibs had barely been speaking since their fight. Not exactly the silent treatment, just speaking only when necessary. If things were better between him and Chels, he'd have come over to see Olive. He adored her. But he made an excuse to bow out when Olive called him.

So for now, it was just Chels and little Olive, people-watching and talking.

Olive was physically a high school student, but mentally she was much older. Both of Olive's parents were killed in a drive-by shooting when she was only five. She was being raised by Great Aunt Grace, which was why sometimes Olive spoke like a seventy-year-old woman and played Bid Whist like a champ.

Chelsea had grown up under Olive's mother, her cousin Jennifer. She always believed that Olive spent too much time with older people, as much as she adored Great Aunt Grace. So from time to time, Chelsea would insist that Olive come spend a few days with her.

She enjoyed the girl much in the same way she used to enjoy her mother. Olive was like her Jennifer in many ways. Whatever intuition Chelsea had, Jennifer had much more. She used to say it was because she was a Virgo and had amazing perception. She couldn't recover stolen bicycles or solve murders like Chelsea, but she'd get these feelings that something was amiss, and usually she was right. Olive had inherited that ability.

"That was Dad who called me this morning. I guess Aunt Grace told him you were here," Chelsea began.

"I already know. Don't get pregnant." Olive sighed in an exasperated teenage way. "Ever since you got pregnant and I got a boyfriend, all I ever hear is lectures about not getting pregnant."

"I heard a lecture today too. Grace and Dad think my pregnancy will make you want to be pregnant," Chelsea said. "I told him you were too smart for that."

"I don't want a baby. But I do want to babysit. Once the baby comes, you won't have time to help Car solve crimes. And I need yaw to find who killed my parents." Olive dropped her head. Chelsea's sleuthing at dinner had made its way around the family. But that was just a fluke.

She put her arm around Olive's shoulder. "I'm sure those guys are already dead, baby cousin. Drug guys just take turns killing each other." It was believed at the time that Jennifer and Marcus were never the intended targets. Sadly, they just happened to be standing in their driveway when some rival drug dealers decided to shoot at the house next door. What Chelsea didn't say was that Carter kept the Jennifer French open homicide file on his desk. Every few months he'd check for new leads on the case. He would love nothing more than to find the men that had killed his favorite cousin.

"Hey," she said, changing the subject, "tell me about this boyfriend? What's his name?"

Olive's face lit up. "Kevin. He's a senior, he's on the basketball team and he never tells me to do my hair." That last line was said triumphantly, due to Olive's resistance against beauty salons. She preferred to braid her hair at home in front of a television— that is, when she felt like combing it. Oftentimes, it was just a big black afro with frosted blonde tips. "He never gets haircuts. He says the barbershop is just filled with old dudes talking about who's the best between Tupac or Biggie, and complaining about everything WE like to listen to. So lame," she chuckled.

"Then I already know Aunt Grace hates him," Chelsea said. Kevin with no haircut standing next to Olive with no perm must have made Grace shiver. She was old school and believed that Black children should look perfect, adorned in only ironed clothing, shiny heads, and shoes without scuffs, lest white people think they are not good enough. Olive, like so many millennials, worked actively to rebel against that kind of thinking.

"She do. She won't even let him in the house. So lately, we've been hanging out at his crib," she replied. "His mom is super cool and she don't care what we do."

Chelsea didn't like the sound of that. "What do you mean, she don't care what you do? You're not in the house alone with this boy, are you?"

"No!" Olive shot back in annoyance. "She be there. She just really only care about her boyfriend. He gets all her attention. At first Kevin didn't like him, but when he figured out how easy it was to sneak out the house, he got over it."

Chelsea stared at Olive with a raised eyebrow. She was beginning to understand why Aunt Grace didn't like young Kevin. She wanted to discuss where Kevin went when he snuck out, but being a police officer's sister had rubbed off on her, and she decided to go in another direction. "What's his mother's name? And the boyfriend? I'm gonna have Car run a check on them."

Olive's arms exploded above her head. "Oh, my God! Why are you tripping? His momma is cool," she implored.

"What about her boyfriend? I don't like him," Chelsea quipped, as much as she hated to think she might be turning into Ray and Grace.

"I don't either. Something about him is," Olive paused to find the right word, "oily. Like he can slide his way through anything."

Chelsea smiled. That was something Jennifer would have said. "I hate when he even talk to me." she continued. "The other day, he stopped me walking into the house to show me where the spare key was, in case I needed it. I don't live there, why would I need it? He said I was a member of the family now, and I may need to get in the house one day. Just in case. I rolled my eyes and told him to stop talking to me."

Chelsea was certain that if Olive rolled her eyes and told the man to stop talking, it was not with the calm reserve she had now. It was probably disrespectful and loud. Little Olive had some anger management issues. Chelsea and Carter weren't doctors, but they attributed it to the tragic loss of her parents. She had a reason to be angry.

Unfortunately, sometimes Olive's anger came out the wrong way to the wrong people, like teachers, principals, social workers, and any other adults she didn't like. She'd never admit it, but it was almost a certainty that Olive spoke horribly to the momma's boyfriend. And Chelsea's interest in this family was now piqued. She sat attentively while Olive told her everything she knew about Kevin's mom and her boyfriend.

"She's a craps dealer at MGM. I know she got money because she got a mink coat in her closet. But Kevin said she got the hookup at the pawn shop inside the casino. She got him a PS4 for like, a hundred dollars. I guess she got her mink on the low and some diamond earrings that she keeps in the freezer." Olive took a swig of pop.

"The mink is dope, Chels. It's real long with a hood and it feels like heaven. Kevin let me try it on one day when she wasn't home."

Chelsea hoped that was the extent of the sneaking around Olive and Kevin were into. Better they play in clothes than take them off.

The coat sounded expensive. The first thing Miss Madeleine had bought after she hit the lottery was a mink coat. It was also long and hooded. Chelsea knew a coat like that was probably around fifteen grand. The casino employees were known to earn good money and work long hours. A hard-working woman with a friend inside the pawn shop wasn't an unreasonable explanation for those luxury items.

"Jimmy, that's the boyfriend, used to cut hair. He don't anymore, but he still does cuts for his friends. Sometimes they come to the house. They be loud in the basement, drinking and smoking. As soon as we see them coming, we just leave. We go across the street and sit in the park," Olive paused with an embarrassed grin, "and hold hands."

Chelsea smiled with her. It was definitely time for someone to have a sex talk with Olive. And more than just the "don't get pregnant" speech.

Her mind drifted for a moment as she pictured Aunt Grace trying to talk to Olive with a bible and a youth minister. There'd be some sort of hellfire in the conversation.

Carter would take Olive down to the precinct and show her mugshots. Specifically, those of boys that looked like they were decent, upstanding citizens, but in actuality were convicted of violent crimes. The Scared Virgin method, as he explained it to Chelsea. A lot of officers used it on their daughters. 'He looks like a nice boy. But he isn't. He's a killer.' Somewhere between eternal damnation and mistrust of all men, was the right talk for Olive.

Chelsea knew she would have to do it. And that's when she heard Olive say, "He gave me the alarm code. So I said, 'Didn't I tell you to stop talking to me?' And he was like, 'In case of emergency, you need to know how to get in. You're family now.' I said, 'Mother fu...'" Olive's true nature was cut off by Chelsea.

"Wait! What? Say that again." Chelsea didn't want to admit that she hadn't heard the last part of Olive's story because she was daydreaming about giving her a sex talk.

"Last Thursday, me and Kevin went to this skating party that was raffling off Drake tickets—which we didn't win. All them radio station contests be rigged. But anyway, I didn't want Aunt Grace to drop me off because she would've been trying to come with me. Me and Kevin wanted to catch the bus. We decided I would meet him at the bus stop. But before Kevin showed up, Jimmy comes walking up the street, stops, and gives me the alarm code."

"And that's when you called him a MF?" Chelsea asked. Olive nodded. "Did you tell Kevin what happened?"

Olive twisted her face. "I meant to. I told him I was tired of Jimmy and his stupid conversations. But before I could say anything else, Kevin kissed me. And then the bus came. And we kissed the whole ride."

"Come on, Olive!" Chelsea was annoyed at her teenage pleasure. "You can kiss anytime! Can't you see what Jimmy is doing? You don't turn your back on the oily man!" She paused. "Where does Kevin live?"

39

"Seven Mile and Outer Drive. Why? Is that where we're going?" Olive's face perked up. "In your car?"

"No. You know I'll never drive that car," Chelsea responded in reference to the previously-owned vehicle Miss Madeleine had given to her after becoming a woman of wealth and leisure. She considered it a guilt gift, and from the day it came delivered (big red bow and all), it had sat in Chelsea's garage beneath a grey polycotton car cover.

"Well, can I have it?" Olive begged. "Please. What's the use of it just sitting in your garage?"

"I promised Dad I wouldn't sell it or give it away." Chelsea hated the car and all it stood for. It was almost as if Maddy had been rewarded for stealing someone's husband. Carter had forgiven her. Chelsea had not. And she was okay walking for her principles. But Snap rarely let that happen. Too bad he was at work.

Olive asked, "Well then, how are we getting there? It's too far to walk in your condition. Lyft?"

"Yes," Chelsea responded, though deep in thought. She was piecing together everything Olive had told her about Kevin's family.

"You would rather pay money than drive your own car?" Olive's annoyance was tempered with a little wasted manipulation.

She wasn't going to talk Chelsea into driving.

"Yup. I'm going to get my purse and change my shoes. Call Kevin and tell him we're on our way. But don't tell him what you just told me. He'll just be confused. Then call Carter and tell him to meet us there."

"Why can't you call Carter?" Olive asked.

Because Chelsea was still angry with her brother. "Never mind." Chelsea stood up and walked into the house. She picked her phone up from the coffee table and dialed Carter as she made her way to her bedroom in the back of the house. The phone rang several times before Carter answered. Chelsea cradled the phone between her neck and chin while she laced up her pink Nike Air Max gym shoes, the ones her obstetrician had recommended she wear to take the strain off her back and legs. But Chels considered them good shoes for fighting.

"What's up, Chels?" Carter said.

"Olive's boyfriend's momma's boyfriend is getting ready to rob her blind if he hasn't already. And he's trying to set Olive up to take the fall. I'm on my way over there. Meet us. It might get ugly." She hung up the phone. She didn't have time to explain everything to Carter who never saw things the way they actually were.

Chelsea stood in the doorway, locking both her front door locks. She glanced down the porch steps at Olive, who was now standing in front of the house looking for the Lyft car. Chelsea made her descent down the steps.

"The car will be here in two minutes. Why are we going over there?" Olive asked.

"You'll find out soon enough. Do me a favor. Text Carter the address." She paused. "Now that you're in love, Ollie, there's something you should know about men."

Olive blushed. "What?" It was like she was expecting something juicy.

"They lie. All the time. They lie when they have to, they lie when they don't. They lie just to lie." Chelsea watched the dejected look on Olive's face. "And the best way to catch a man in a lie is to let him talk. He'll eventually tell on himself. Just let him talk."

The two ladies stood in front of the house for exactly two minutes, and then the Lyft car arrived.

Chapter Eight

Kevin opened the front door with a broad grin. "You must be the famous cousin Chelsea I keep hearing about." He opened the screen door for the two ladies. He kissed Olive's cheek as she passed him, then closed the door and led everyone into the living room.

"Hello, Kevin. I'm pretty sure I don't want to know what you've heard," Chelsea replied. Refusing to move to Boca and live with the parents, refusing to drive the guilt car, working at the grocery store and getting pregnant by a convict had given Chelsea's family plenty to discuss. She could only imagine what version of her life Kevin had been told.

"Well, it's still nice to meet you," he said charmingly. But that hair. Was everywhere. As Chelsea drank in his giant clumps of hair, she determined the boy probably hadn't had a haircut or even a comb in at least 3 years. The back stuck straight up and out, but the front was longer and kind of fell off to the side. But, he was a handsome kid, and Chelsea understood Olive's attraction.

"Even though," he began, "I have no idea why you're here."

Chelsea jumped right in. "So, Jimmy cuts hair in the basement? What else do they do down there?"

Kevin seemed rather startled at the line of questioning. "How do you...? I wouldn't know. As soon as I hear the sound of clippers, I am out!" Seeing the disappointed look on Chelsea's face, he continued, "He's always saying he's gonna tie me down and cut my hair. At first I thought he was playing, but he's kind of an a-hole. So, just to be safe, I leave."

"Where's your mother's fur coat?" Chelsea continued to just steamroll through the conversation without regard for anyone else's confusion.

"It's upstairs in her closet. Why are you asking these questions?" he said, in a man-of-the-house kind of way.

"I don't think so. But go check," Chelsea responded. "Check on those earrings too, while you're at it." But before Kevin could leave the room, a woman, obviously his mother, entered and gently blocked her son's path.

"Wait just one minute please, son. I didn't know we had company. Hello, Olive. Who is this woman bossing my son around in my house?" she asked.

Chelsea looked upon the woman and smiled amiably. She was taller than Chelsea and thin, very attractive with long black hair, which she wore in a braid that lay against one shoulder, and bright brown eyes that danced even when she was annoyed. Like now.

"Hello. I'm the cousin. Chelsea French," she said, extending her hand.

"The crazy pregnant one?" she replied.

Chelsea sighed.

"Well, half-right, anyway. I'm gonna need to sit." She rubbed her stomach and plopped on the sofa. "Sorry, didn't catch your name."

"Karen," the lady said in a controlled tone. "You already know my son, Kevin."

"Yes. He's a very handsome boy. Kevin, be good and go check on your mother's things. Ollie, go with him," Chelsea repeated. She understood Karen's confusion, but found it quite tiresome. She certainly didn't take a Lyft all this way just to be snapped at by the lady she was trying to save. After the kids darted up the stairs, she asked, "Where's Jimmy?"

Karen became enraged. "Wait a minute!" she said loudly, looking at Chelsea's stomach. "Did you come over here to tell me Jimmy was your baby daddy?"

Chelsea gave a comforting smile, "No, no. This is James's baby." And at that moment she realized that Jimmy could be James. "Not your James, but my James. He's in jail. Not the same guy."

Karen relaxed a little, but still appeared agitated. "Then what the hell do you want?"

Olive came back into the living room alone and shook her head. Chelsea could hear Kevin opening the freezer and checking on the status of the earrings. He re-entered the room with a solemn face and looked at his mother.

"Momma, your stuff is gone. I know you said not to let Olive try on your coat, but I swear, we put it back. We don't know what happened to it," he said with tears in his eyes. Karen screamed out and took off running up the stairs to see for herself. About ten seconds later, her scream was ten times intensified.

Chelsea put her head in her hands. A headache was coming on. Olive came and sat next to her.

"Car just sent me a text," Olive whispered in Chelsea's ear. "He said he'd be here in a couple of minutes and not to let you do anything crazy. Maybe we should go."

Chelsea was sitting in a strange woman's house getting ready to accuse her boyfriend of grand larceny. The crazy ship had already sailed. "Tell him to hurry up," was Chelsea's response.

Karen ran back down the stairs and straight at Chelsea. "Do you have my coat?"

46

"No, Karen. And I really was hoping I could get here before it was stolen. I was trying to prevent this."

"What do you know about this?" she yelled. Turning toward Olive, "If you took my coat, little girl...I'm calling the police!"

Olive finally spoke up, "My cousin Carter is on his way here, Miss Karen. He is the police."

Karen's hysteria subsided for a moment. Defeated, she sat down in the chair next to the sofa. She looked at Chelsea. "What's going on?"

A gentle rap on the screen door let Chelsea know that Carter had arrived. She sighed in relief.

"That's my cousin," Olive said, jumping up to open the door for him. Carter walked in with trepidation. Seeing Chelsea, he gave her a disapproving look. "Chels, what's going on?"

"Your family came in my house uninvited, and some kind of way my fur coat and my diamond earrings came up missing! I want them back or I'm pressing charges!" Karen's anger had been reinvigorated. She jumped up.

Carter, of course, was no stranger to walking in on disputes, being an officer of the Detroit Police Department for several years. He'd seen it all when he was a beat cop. He knew how to calm people.

"Ma'am, I am Detective Carter French. And if my sister's done anything wrong, I will take care of it, I assure you. But I need to hear why she asked me to come. Is that all right?" He was moving very slowly toward the couch. Karen nodded, and Carter sat next to Chelsea.

"Olive was telling me about her new boyfriend and how she comes over here to hang out. She told me about your coat and your earrings and Kevin's PS4, which is probably also missing...and your boyfriend, Jimmy," Chelsea turned to look at Carter, "whom she described as 'oily'."

Carter looked at Olive. "Oily?" he asked, then stood up.

"Where is this Jimmy?" he asked Karen directly.

"Ain't nothing wrong with Jimmy! That's my man! He loves me! He ain't got nothing to do with this! That's my family! My stuff was fine until yo family got here!"

Carter looked back at Chelsea. "When you arrived, the coat was gone? What happened, Chels?"

"Yeah! What happened to my stuff?" Karen yelled.

But Carter wasn't asking Chelsea to explain herself.

"I need to talk to Jimmy," she responded. "One thing is for sure, he ain't as dumb as he looks."

48

"You know him?" Carter asked, confused.

"Never met him. Just looking at those pictures of him." Chelsea pointed to several candid shots of Karen and Jimmy posing at different nightclubs that were framed and sitting on the mantel. There was usually a man at the clubs with a camera selling pictures. Jimmy and Karen were obviously good customers. They must've taken pictures every time they went out.

After a few seconds of rustling keys at the back door, Jimmy was in the house. Carter stepped behind Olive and whispered for her to stay in front of him. He didn't want Jimmy to see his badge and gun.

Jimmy bounced up the back steps through the kitchen and into the living room. He was in a good mood. "What's up, family? Did yaw know it's a police car outside? Something must be popping off on the block... Oh, we got company. Hi, I'm Jimmy." He reached his hand out to Carter, who did not extend his in return. Jimmy retracted his hand. "Olive, you in trouble?"

Jimmy was much better-looking in person than in the photographs. He was of a light brown complexion with wavy black hair that, of course, was perfectly cut. His linen shirt fit nicely against his slender yet muscular frame, with rolled sleeves revealing tattoos on his forearms. And he was easily ten years younger than Karen.

Chelsea had motioned to Olive to remain quiet. But Karen jumped right in.

"All my stuff is missing! My coat and my earrings!" she cried.

"And my PS4!" Kevin joined in. He had checked after Chelsea's cryptic reference.

"What?" Jimmy reacted dramatically. "We got robbed? When? How did they get in?"

"Ain't nobody broke into my house," Karen said defiantly.

"It was an inside job." She turned to Olive when she said the last part. This made Chelsea want to smack Karen.

"Awww, Olive. Not you? How you gon' do us like that? We took you in," Jimmy lamented. "Are you her foster parents? Yaw gotta make this right." He shook his head at Chelsea. "Cause this, this ain't right."

"These are her cousins," Karen said. "They trying to blame it on you!"

Jimmy stepped back in awe. "Me? Olive! You know better." He sighed heavily before turning to Karen. "Baby, I should've told you this earlier, but I saw Olive with your spare key last week. She said Kevin told her she could use it to get in. I didn't think it was right, but I figured he was trying to sneak his little girlfriend in the house and I had no idea she was gonna steal."

50

Olive reared up, hands in air and she was about to say something Carter knew would be acidic, so he put his hand over her mouth and pulled her back. Chelsea gave Olive a sympathetic eye. "Just let him talk, baby cuz." Olive calmed down.

"I told you I wasn't comfortable with you bringing her in this house!" Karen began to yell at Kevin. "A girl with no family will do anything to survive! And you showed her my coat? What were you thinking?"

Kevin crossed in front of his mother and walked toward Olive, who by now had tears streaming down her face. "I don't think Olive would steal from me." He said, taking her hand. Chelsea was secretly pleased with the courageous and loyal gesture. Poor Kevin had no idea how the Frenches would've forever hated him, had he not stood up for her. They were especially protective of Olive.

"Olive has a family that loves her very much. We wouldn't be here if we didn't," Carter said in a calm voice. "I don't think there is any proof Olive stole anything. First off, when is the last time you saw your coat, ma'am?"

Karen thought for a second. "I keep it in a garment bag at the back of my closet. Most of the time, I don't pay it any attention. But I knew Kevin and Olive had played with it because they didn't zip the bag up. I noticed it Wednesday night when I got home from work, around eleven thirty.

That's when I told him to stay out of my shit! I've been working the afternoon shift, so I'm gone most evenings, but I'm home during the day."

"Thursday night, me and Olive went skating. She never came to the house. We met at the bus stop," Kevin chimed in. "And Friday night, I was here alone until you came home."

"So it must have been last night. Kevin sent me a text around four that he was leaving the house and that he'd probably spend the night at his best friend's. I worked until midnight. Got home around twelve thirty in the morning. Jimmy came home after two. House was empty for hours. It had to be her!" The evening, before Aunt Grace and Olive picked Chelsea up, the three had dinner and had gone back to Chelsea's house. Aunt Grace left around ten, but Olive was never out of Chelsea's sight. But knowing Olive was innocent and proving that Jimmy was guilty were not the same thing.

"Hey Car, a single woman works hard and buys some nice stuff. She wants to protect them, so she gets an alarm for her house. Is it your experience that she would leave a key in the driveway where anybody could find it?" Now it was Chelsea's turn to be sarcastic.

"No, actually, it's the exact opposite. People with alarm systems almost never have keys lying around outside. Especially in Detroit," he responded resolutely.

"Was it your idea to keep a key outside, or Jimmy's?"

Chelsea directed her question to Karen, who got a strange look in her eye.

"It was his, but that was because Kevin kept locking himself out. That doesn't mean anything! A lot of people keep hide-a-keys! Stop trying to put this on Jimmy! He don't even need to sneak in. He lives here," she shot back.

Jimmy reacted, "Naw, don't try to blame this on me! Yaw trying to protect yaw own!"

"Well, it had to be one of you." Chelsea turned to Kevin.

"Tell me exactly what happened yesterday afternoon when you decided to leave."

"I was on the phone with Olive. I heard Jimmy and his friends come in. At first they were just talking, but when I heard those clippers, I was out the door," Kevin said.

Jimmy smiled and nudged Karen playfully. "I always tease the boy about cutting his hair, but I would never do it if he didn't want me to. Baby, you know me."

"You wouldn't have to. All you had to do was make him think that you might, and just the sound of the clippers would be enough to get him out the house. Momma was at work and you had the place to yourself. You told Olive where the key was and gave her the alarm code. She was your patsy," said Chelsea.

Karen reacted when she heard the last part. "Alarm code? Why would you give her my alarm code?"

Jimmy put his hands up. "I didn't. That's not what happened. That little girl is lying on me, baby! I SAW her with a piece of paper that had the code on it. I asked her how she got it and AGAIN, she said Kevin gave it to her. I swear, I never thought she was gonna steal from you!"

Kevin turned to Olive in surprise. "You got the alarm code to my house?"

"He gave it to me, but I ain't know why!" she protested.

"So you had a key, the code, and you knew Kevin was gone. All you had to do was wait for Jimmy to leave. That's all I need to know!" Karen was getting amped up again.

"Olive was with my Great Aunt Grace last night. And if you say Grace was in on it, I'm knocking you out," Chelsea said with too much calm to be a bluff.

"Chelsea!" Carter interjected. "She will not hit you. I promise. But everybody's movements are accounted for, except yours, Jimmy." Carter took this moment to finally step from behind Olive. His badge and gun seemed to shake Jimmy up.

"You the police? Uh, well, I cut my boy's hair, then we grabbed a bite to eat and hit the club. I stayed there until two and then got home about half an hour later, like Karen said," Jimmy responded.

Chelsea figured he was the Saturday night clubbing type of guy. The clothes, the pictures...the pictures.

"What club?" Chelsea asked, pulling her phone out. She went to the popular Picture Me Clubbing website. A group of photographers that went around to all the party spots in Detroit took candid shots of Detroit's socialites and party people. But instead of the old-school printed photos, the next day the partygoers could just go to the website and download high resolution pictures. Wasn't technology wonderful?

"Club Excess. My homie had a birthday party. We turned up real good. Plenty of people saw me there," he confidently responded.

"I think you two should cool it. This relationship ain't working out for me. We ain't have no problems until she came around. And I don't care if her uncle is a cop, I'm about to call the real police and get her little tail arrested! In fact, all yaw can get out of my house!" Karen was agitated and moving threateningly toward Carter and Olive. Carter put his hands out to block her as she roared at him. "Get out! Get out now!"

"Karen, calm down. You might want to see this," Chelsea said, holding up her phone.

"What is it?" Jimmy asked.

"Just the proof that you were at the club. You took a ton of pictures," Chelsea responded.

"Right. Because that's where I was. Like I told you." he said arrogantly.

"I really was hoping I could prove you was lying by finding these pictures. But I found something way better." Chelsea took her two fingers, sliding them across the screen of her phone to increase the size of the picture. She handed the phone to Karen who reluctantly took it.

"Jimmy was at the party. Took a couple of pictures with a very pretty lady. Who...also has a pair of expensive diamond earrings." Chelsea was smug. "What are the odds?" she said to Carter.

Carter shrugged. "I guess he is as dumb as he looks."

Chapter Nine

After a short physical altercation between Karen and Jimmy, the arrival of an ambulance and another squad car, the Frenches and Kevin stood in front of Kevin's house. Jimmy was arrested and Karen had to go to the precinct to file a formal complaint. Carter had offered to keep an eye on Kevin for her. Chelsea had already called a Lyft to take her back.

"Chelsea, I'll take you home."

"It's okay. Why don't you take the kids for a bite to eat?"

Carter nodded, barely making eye contact with his sister.

"What's wrong with yaw?" Olive asked, her apparent intuition kicking in.

"Nothing, cousin. Let Carter show you his new cruiser. He'll let you play with the siren." Chelsea forced a smile.

Olive wasn't buying it. "I hate when yaw fight."

Before Chelsea could deny anything, her car pulled up. She decided to let it go. "See you back at the house, Ollie."

Chapter Ten

Two days after Chelsea bum-rushed her way into Karen's home, Olive and Kevin sat in Chelsea's living room. Chelsea had just gotten off work and arrived home to find the teenagers deep in an Arrow/Flash marathon, debating the merits of each show. Chelsea was exhausted after eight hours on her pregnant feet and had every intention of being asleep in the next fifteen minutes.

"What do you want me to call you?" Kevin asked as she passed the twosome.

"Not the crazy pregnant one, please," Chelsea responded. "Chels is good."

"Thanks for helping my mom get her stuff back. She's still mad at the way you did it, but I think she's grateful too. Can you believe he still had all of it in his car?" said Kevin.

"He didn't think she'd miss a fur coat in the middle of summer. He figured he had time to hock the stuff out of town. Your mom's pawn shop friends would have found anything he sold locally. They keep records and video. Jimmy was probably working on an excuse to go to Ohio or Indiana. And he thought blaming Olive would work. And it might have, if he hadn't cheated on your mom."

"What was it that gave him away?" Olive asked. "It was happening to me and I didn't see it. I just thought he was a pervo."

Chelsea sat down in her father's old easy chair. "This one time when we were kids, your mother took me and Car to the state fair. And we came across this guy doing card tricks. For a dollar, he'd shuffle the cards and if you could find the queen he'd pay you two. Carter thought he was so smart, he was sure he could beat the guy. Jennifer told us not to trust him. Said he looked oily. But Carter didn't listen and he lost all the money he had." She laughed. "So you see, baby cuz, it all started with a word."

Chelsea stood up and headed for her bedroom. She looked at the love-crazy teens and knew she should talk to Olive about sex soon. But in her fatigue, all she could manage was, "Hey Ollie, don't get pregnant."

Olive heaved an embarrassed sigh as Chelsea swung her bedroom door shut. She immediately opened it back up again. She was beginning to think like a parent.

Chapter Eleven

"Are you glowing?" Snap said as he opened the passenger side door of his large black Cadillac Escalade. "Or are you sweating? I can't tell." He helped her up to the running board.

Chelsea struggled to maintain her balance as she fell into the passenger seat. "Me neither. It's so hot today." She closed the door and affixed her seatbelt across her expanding belly.

Snap always picked Chelsea up from work on Mondays. It was his regular off day and he usually didn't do too much except catch up on his DVR, grab a haircut, get a carwash and maybe go buy gym shoes if something new was out. He knew that he wasn't really going to marry Chelsea, but as long as Ray French believed it, he was more than willing to do his share to take care of her. Ray had called several times in the last few weeks to make sure Snap was doing right by his daughter.

Being the only child of two only children, Snap was lonely, having no siblings or cousins. Moving next door to the Frenches had changed everything. Carter was two years older and too bossy, but Chelsea was his age and perfectly amiable since their first meeting. It was the first day of sixth grade, and

Snap had stood on the porch, not really sure how to get to school, but knowing that his next-door neighbors (whom he hadn't actually met yet) would be walking past him soon. He decided he would follow them at a safe distance.

Carter had come out of the house, going on about being an eighth grader and telling Chelsea that he wouldn't be able to talk to her anymore. Mrs. French stepped on the porch, ordering Carter to be nice to his sister on her first day. Chelsea bounced out of the house, not paying Carter any attention. She jumped off the porch and did a solid landing on the sidewalk. She mimicked an Olympic dismount with both arms stretched above her head.

"By the end of the day, you'll be the one trying to talk to me," she'd told her brother with certainty.

He poked his lips out and the two began to walk down the street. Chelsea looked up at Snap and said, "Are you coming or what?"

Snap had smiled and run off his own porch to join them.

Carter sighed, "How many sixth graders do I have to babysit?"

Chelsea jumped right back, "You're not babysitting; we are." Snap laughed. Then Chelsea introduced herself, "I'm Chelsea, and this is my stupid brother, Carter. He thinks he's gonna be the king of the school just because he's in the eighth grade."

"I'm Devin," Snap said shyly.

"That ain't what we heard your momma calling you," Carter said. "She was yelling, Snap! Sit yo behind down somewhere and stop all that jumping around."

The children laughed.

"I was doing flips off the steps. She got mad," Snap said, still laughing. "That's what my mom calls me. But my name is Devin."

So Devin would futilely spend his first day of school introducing himself by his proper name, only to have Chelsea call him "Snap" and giggle. Overall, the first day at a new school wasn't so bad. He had made a few friends, including Chelsea, who he thought was the prettiest girl in his class. And he didn't have any homework. That meant he could go home and play video games before dinner.

He and Chelsea stood under a tree in front of the junior high, waiting for the popular Carter to join them so they could go home. Chelsea was getting impatient; she wanted to get home in time to watch TRL.

"Here he comes, finally," Chelsea said, annoyed.

Carter walked out of the school holding hands with a very pretty eighth grader. It looked like they were a couple. Chelsea rolled her eyes when she saw them together.

"I didn't know Carter had a girlfriend," Snap said, looking at Chelsea's frown. "You don't like her?"

"That's Chantay. And I think she's fake. She wouldn't talk to him all summer and now they go together? If she calls the house, I'm hanging up on her," she said.

Snap laughed as they continued to watch Carter with his new girl. He looked happy holding her hand and walking slowly. That was, until Michael Simpson ran up behind him and pushed him so hard, he fell down. Chantay cried out, and in a few seconds, a circle of students had formed around Carter and Michael, egging on a fight. Michael was saying something about Chantay being HIS girlfriend.

Michael and Carter had years of bad blood between them. Michael had stolen Carter's bike, and they had fought many times. Even Mrs. French and Ms. Simpson had occasion to hurl a few obscenities at each other in the street over the boys. Chelsea was able to outsmart Michael, but it was a well-known fact that Carter could not outfight Michael.

Chelsea ran over to the circle, ready to jump in and fight with her brother. She pressed her way into the center, getting pulled back by some of Michael's friends and having to push them off of her. By the time she reached the inner circle, her face was red and she was steaming mad. She ran right at Michael, who floored her immediately. Carter stepped in, screaming about his sister, and Michael balled up his fist to punch him. But Snap stepped between them.

"Who is you?" Michael asked defiantly.

"These are my friends. If you hurt them, I'm gonna have to hurt you. I been in karate since I was five. You don't want none of this," Snap said confidently.

Some of the kids began to laugh, but others, including Michael's friends, began to yell out for a fight.

"Don't nobody care about your karate! This is the hood!" Michael taunted. Snap stepped closer to him and was taller by an inch. "You little sixth grader," Michael said and he tried to push Snap out of the way.

But Snap had studied karate for the last seven years. He twisted Michael's arm behind his back and forced him down on his knees. The crowd was electric. For years, Michael had beat people up, but it was just street fighting. This was a display of real skill.

"I can break your arm right now if I wanted to," Snap said arrogantly. "But I don't. This is just a sample." He let Michael up.

Michael had watched years of professional wrestling and thought that he, too, could pull off a fancy attack move. He tried to get Snap in a headlock, but Snap maneuvered out of it and, for a second time, had Michael down on the ground with everyone laughing in the background.

"You out of your league, man. Just leave us alone," Snap warned.

Michael was a bully. And bullies didn't listen to warnings.

He jumped up and tried to swing his fist at Snap who just ducked for a second, and then with a boxer's stance, he socked Michael across the jaw, and Michael went down. He didn't get up the third time. "I used to box too," Snap said.

Everyone began to cheer for Snap until the principal broke through the crowd, grabbed both boys, and dragged them back into the school. A couple of teachers had also come outside and were yelling for everyone to go home. As the crowd dispersed, Chelsea looked for Carter, who had walked off with Chantay. But Chelsea wasn't done with her. She ran over to them.

"So are you Michael's girlfriend?" she yelled.

"I mean, he WAS my boyfriend. But I broke up with him because he was talking to Laurencia and me at the same time," Chantay said.

It would be a year before Chelsea would have her first boyfriend. She had never been kissed or even courted. But she knew no girl that liked Michael would also like Carter. The two boys were as different as night and day. Chelsea suspected Chantay was using Carter to make Michael jealous. And she said as much to Chantay. Carter tried to defend Chantay, but Chelsea blew him off.

"Shut up, Carter! You can be stupid if you want to! But she playin' you!" And with that, Chelsea stormed off down the street toward home.

"I gotta go," Carter said abruptly to Chantay, who was still fussing. He knew that Ray French would kill him if Chelsea walked all the way home alone. "Call me later?" He took off down the street after his baby sister.

Chantay did not call him later, or ever again. She and Michael were back together the next day.

About an hour-and-a-half later, Snap and his mother pulled into their driveway. The French children were waiting to find out how much trouble Snap was in. Mrs. French wanted to say something to Snap's mom on his behalf. She was happy Carter hadn't gotten beat up again. But Snap's mom didn't seem mad when she got out of her car. Just inconvenienced.

"You made me miss Oprah! Always trying to show off. Shoulda never put you in that karate class," she fussed as she walked into her house.

66

Snap looked up at Carter and Chelsea. "Wassup?" he asked calmly, as if he had just woken up from a nap.

"What happened?" Chelsea asked anxiously.

"We got suspended. But just for one day. Principal said since it was my first day at a new school, he'd give me a break."

"Aren't you gonna get in trouble with your mom?"

"Naw, she ain't mad. I told her I had to stand up for my friends," Snap said walking toward his own house. "She'll probably make me help her unpack boxes. There's like, a million of them."

The next day after school, Carter and Chelsea also helped unpack their boxes. It was the least they could do for their new bodyguard. It didn't take Snap long to have a reputation in the neighborhood for his formidable fighting skills. And his loyalty to the French children kept Carter safe from Michael Simpson well through high school.

As for Chantay, she gave Michael his first two children before she was twenty. Seventeen years, four babies and thirty pounds later, she would be the manager of the very Big Jack's Chicken Shack that Snap was pulling into.

Chapter Twelve

"I'm hungry. You want something, preggers?" he asked.

As Chelsea and Chantay had never resolved their differences over the years, she wasn't about to trust her meal to that woman. "No, thanks. I'd rather eat dirt. I'll stay in the car," Chelsea said.

"That's probably exactly what you'd end up with!" Snap laughed out. "She'd just sweep it off the floor and put it in your mashed potato bowl."

"She must like you if you feel safe enough to eat here. Maybe you should date her." Cheslea scoffed, knowing that Michael Simpson would sooner walk home from his deployment to Iraq before he would let Snap anywhere near his children. "I'll be back, big head." Snap jumped out of the car and ran into the Shack.

Chelsea sighed because she was hungry. But she would never let herself eat any meal Chantay had a hand in preparing. The rivalry between Chelsea and Chantay only began in the sixth grade, but endured the test of time. For a while in high school, it was a guarantee that if those two both showed up at the same field trip, party, or graduation, there would be a fight with fists, usually broken up by a teacher, random parent, and in one case, several mall security officers. And while adulthood had matured the ladies enough to stop publicly fighting (the last fight, they were twenty-one at a neighborhood bar), the animosity between them lingered.

As Chelsea sat in the car waiting for Snap to return, she tried to remember what exactly had set off their seventeen-year feud. And it wasn't that Chantay had used Carter. She was the first of many women that would take advantage of him. He attracted that type.

About ten minutes later, Snap came back out with a bag of Big Jack's famous lemon pepper wings. He opened the car door and tossed Chelsea the bag.

"Hold this. I'm about to get this girl's number."

"What girl?" Chelsea asked.

"Chantay introduced me to her friend, Janeen. I wanna call her. Is that okay with you? We not really engaged, remember?" He smiled.

"Ray French betta' not find out you cheatin' on me," Chelsea teased. "Hurry up."

Snap closed the door and walked back toward the front of the Shack. Janeen met him outside with a coy giggle and flirtatious push. "You so crazy, Devin," she laughed.

Chelsea watched as Snap pulled out his cell phone and handed it to Janeen for her to add her contact information. She looked like the kind of girl that had an excessive Instagram name like, @JaneenStuntinOnYouHoesAndHaters. She was pretty, in an overdone, trying-to-be-Beyoncé kind of way. She wore too much weave and had on too much makeup and artificial eyelashes that Chelsea could see from the car that was parked twenty feet away. But Snap had a type. All of his girlfriends looked like Janeen. Not ugly, just needed a good face-washing and a dose of Nikki Giovanni's Natural Woman. He didn't care how they looked in person, just how they looked in pictures. He liked to show off his collection of hotties around the GM Stamping Plant, where he worked. And what was too much for the naked eye was perfect for the camera. The guys ogling the pics at the job would think Janeen was "flawless".

Just as Snap hugged Janeen and began walking back toward the car, Chantay came running out the door.

"Snap! Come back!" she yelled out. "Somebody stole all the money!"

Janeen jumped back and screamed, "What?"

Snap turned around and ran into the restaurant, pushing past Chantay and Janeen. Snap was still the hero. He expected to find masked assailants running out the back door or something like that. He was disappointed to see only the confused fry cook staring back at him. He slowly walked back outside.

"What you talkin' about, Chantay?"

"One of YAW took the deposit money!" she accused. "Right before you came in I put an envelope with seventeen hundred dollars in my purse to go make a deposit at the bank. I kicked it wit' you, gave your order to Deontay, went in my office to take a call and when I came back out, the money was gone!"

"Maybe you misplaced it," Snap offered the distraught woman.

"No!" she screamed. "I didn't. One of YAW took it! Now I gotta call the police! I'm gonna get fired!" She shook her head and walked back inside the restaurant. Janeen followed her, protesting for her innocence.

Snap looked up at the car and saw Chelsea smugly typing into her phone, trying to pretend she couldn't hear what was going on. But he knew better. He also knew Chelsea could figure this out.

During their senior year of high school, the homecoming fund had come up missing. The popular Snap had been accused by Amber Miller, because she said he was the last person in the office where it had been taken from. But really, it was because he had refused her invitation to be his date for the dance. He rushed to room 201 where several students, including Chelsea, were serving detention. She managed to sneak out and into the hallway. Snap had about four minutes to explain the situation before Chelsea was dragged back into the classroom. An hour later, Snap was in the principal's office, facing the homecoming committee, accused of a crime he didn't commit. Chelsea charged into the office (without knocking), dragging Whitney Barron, head cheerleader behind her. Confused and reluctant, Whitney told the principal that the cheerleaders had locked the gym doors during practice while they worked on their secret routine. Which meant that Amber Miller must have been lying when she said she was in the gym decorating at the time the money had come up missing. Amber had immediately crumbled and confessed. And Snap was free to win homecoming king and take the busty Melanie Hearn as his date.

Snap walked over to the car and opened the door.
"Come on, Scooby Doo. We need you."

'Scooby Doo' was the nickname the senior class had given Chelsea after she recovered the homecoming fund.

"What do you expect me to do? I didn't see anything," 'Scooby' said, never looking up from her Facebook app.

"Chelsea. We need your special set of skills," he said, mimicking Liam Neeson in their favorite movie, Taken.

"I ain't helping her! Let's go!"

"I think I'm a suspect, though."

"Please! We all know you ain't take the money! Chantay knows better than to blame you!"

"She's gonna lose her job, Chels."

Chelsea shrugged, still not looking up from her phone. Snap quietly stared at her until she did. When she saw his facial expression, she sighed.

"I wouldn't even know what to do."

"Nobody can spot a lie better than you. And somebody, not me, is obviously lying."

Chelsea smacked her lips. "It's probably Chantay."

"Don't be like that, Chels. You're better than this."

No, she wasn't. But Snap thought so. And that was what endeared him to Chelsea. He always saw her in the best light, even when she felt the darkest.

She slowly opened her car door and very carefully climbed out of Snap's giant vehicle. She followed behind him as he led her into the Shack.

Chantay saw Chelsea and her mouth dropped. But she didn't say a word. What could she say? Chelsea had outsmarted Michael too many times to be doubted.

Big Jack's Chicken Shack was like most fast food restaurants. Diners had the option of sitting in uncomfortable vinyl booths or carrying out. There was a self-service soda fountain that sat on one counter with a napkin dispenser, a pile of straws, and about a hundred packets of ketchup. The other counter separated the dining room from the kitchen. There were three cash registers sitting on top of the second counter, but only two of them worked properly. There was a microphone the staff used for special orders to the kitchen. Behind the counter, near the register, Chantay's purse sat, wide open.

"Is that where your purse was?" Chelsea asked at Chantay (she refused to talk to her).

"It was under the register. I put it there after I counted out the deposit. I was getting ready to run to the bank, but I got a call from my district manager in my office. I only left my purse for a few minutes."

"That was dumb," Chelsea jabbed. "Why can't you just look at the camera?"

"Come on, Chels. You know them cameras don't work," Snap jumped in. "Look, it's only one door up here and one door at the back that leads to the alley. It was me, Chantay, Janeen, and that other dude in here. Now, do yo' thang."

Chelsea stood quietly, looking around the room. She didn't want to disappoint Snap, but her "thang" as he called it couldn't just be summoned like a magical power. It was mostly instinct, and usually involved shady people telling lies. These were just fast food workers standing and staring at her.

Janeen was confused by Snap's attention to Chelsea. She obviously had not seen her sitting in his car.

"Is this yo baby mama?" she rudely asked.

"Naw, this is my best friend, Chelsea. Chels, this is Janeen," he said, trying to preemptively avoid any problems between the two ladies. Rarely did he date a girl that Chelsea liked.

"So that ain't yo baby?" she asked again. Snap shook his head. Chelsea turned and looked at the girl. If nails too long for food service was a crime then this girl was definitely guilty. "Where were you when the money came up missing?"

"Huh?" Janeen raised her eyebrow with an attitude. "Why you askin'?"

Chelsea walked to the counter and let Snap explain to Janeen what was going on. She lacked the patience to deal with Chantay and Janeen. There was a swinging door for staff to enter the kitchen.

"Do you mind if I go back here? I'd like to see the whole layout," Chelsea asked.

The fry cook pushed the door open for her and grabbed a hairnet out of a box underneath the counter.

"It's the law," he said, handing it to her.

Chelsea patted her neatly bunned hair to check for any hanging tresses. There was no way she was wearing a hairnet when Chantay and Janeen wore enough collective weave to open a beauty supply store.

"When they wear one, I'll wear one," she said, fanning her hand in the direction of Chantay.

She walked past him and to the back door past the drive through window and the deep fryer where a bag of frozen wings sat adjacent. She could feel the heat from the popping grease as she moved past it. The fryer was very hot. There were boxes with Big Jack's logo stacked from floor to ceiling and plastic bags for carryout orders in an open box by the back door. She pushed open the back door and saw a folding chair sitting alone in the alley surrounded by cigarette butts. It must've been where the employees came for breaks.

She closed the back door, still having no idea how to figure out who the thief was. She knew it wasn't Snap. It might've been Janeen, or the fry cook, or maybe even Chantay had picked up a thing or two after being with Michael Simpson for so many years.

"The money was stolen before we got here," she stated plainly, without any voice inflection.

"How you know?" Chantay asked.

"Because Snap would never steal from you. Stop acting like you don't know him! And he would never let anybody steal from you. And from where your purse is, he could see it from the register where he ordered his food. He stayed in the room to talk to Janeen after he got his food. She followed him outside when you came back to the register. It had to have happened after you claim you took the phone call and before we pulled up," Chelsea explained.

"What you mean 'claim'?" Chantay asked, offended.

Chelsea ignored her because they both knew what she meant by 'claim'. She continued to walk around the kitchen. She was repulsed at how much grease was on the wall. She looked at Deontay, the fry cook.

"What were you doing right before Snap walked in?"

He pointed to a tray of fried chicken sitting under a heat lamp. "Cooking that chicken. Stood right in front of the fryer and didn't move until it was all cooked, including your friend's order. That's how I always do it. I never take my eyes off my fryer."

"That's true. Deontay is my best cook. He takes the chicken very seriously. My customers love him," Chantay vouched. Chelsea nodded as she took a closer look at the chicken. She grabbed a fried wing. It was hot. She blew on it and took a bite before standing face to face with Janeen.

"Where were you right before we got here, Janeen?"

Janeen smacked her lips. "Why is you asking me questions? Who are you to me?"

Chantay answered before Chelsea had a chance, "Answer the question!"

A mildly affronted Janeen rolled her eyes. "I took the garbage outside and called my son's father."

Are yaw still kicking it?" Snap inquired with slight irritation. "You just gave me your phone number. I ain't got time for no crazy baby daddy situations."

"Devin. Focus," Chelsea said pacing calmly as she continued to eat the chicken wing. Her hunger could wait no longer. She was dangerously close to grabbing a side of coleslaw.

"No, I had to make sure he was picking up my son from daycare today. Sometimes he forgets and I have to pay extra. I can show you my phone. It proves what time and how long I talked to him. I didn't touch the money," she pleaded.

Chelsea had worked her way back around to the chicken tray and was about to grab another piece when Deontay handed her a plastic glove and a paper plate.

"Put on the glove and use the tongs," he instructed.

Chelsea looked up at him, preparing to oblige his sanitary request. But she glanced over his shoulder and noticed how clean the wall was. She walked over to the wall.

"Why is this wall so clean, but the other so dirty?" Deontay jumped to respond.

"Because the grease pops in this direction. This wall always catches it, except for when it hits me."

Chelsea walked over to the greasy wall. It was warm to the touch. No doubt from the grease from the last batch he had fried.

"Hot grease would burn. Did you get any burns on this last batch?"

"No," Deontay smiled. "So far no burns."

"Well then, either this warm grease on the wall must have gone around your body, or you weren't standing here frying that delicious chicken the whole time. Chantay, he's lying. Come feel the wall for yourself. How did the grease hit the wall without burning him? He must have stepped away for a few seconds."

Chantay pushed through the swinging door and walked straight to the wall opposite the fryer. She felt the warm grease and looked back at Deontay. He looked at her for a split second, then bolted out the back door, shoving Chelsea out of

79

his way, pushing her into the fryer. She stumbled back and almost fell into the bubbling hot grease. Chantay grabbed her and pulled her back up in the nick of time.

Snap ran out the front door after Deontay.

"He won't get out the parking lot!" he yelled as he cleared the doorway.

But Chantay didn't need Snap to be the hero. After helping Chelsea, she followed Deontay. By the time Snap ran around the building to the alley, Chantay had grabbed Deontay before he could jump the fence and pulled him down to the ground. He was struggling to get away from her, but she punched him in the face so hard, his neck snapped back like a Pez dispenser. Snap came up behind him, grabbed his arms, and held them behind his back. Chantay began searching him until she found the envelope with the deposit money in the bottom pocket of his cargo pants.

Chelsea and Janeen stood in the alley, watching. Snap released Deontay. He pushed back and looked like he wanted to fight. Snap stepped back.

"Dude. Who you trying to fight? You're outnumbered."

"I'll beat you down by myself!" Chantay exclaimed. "I don't need no help!"

As one that had fought Chantay several times over the years, Chelsea was well aware of her rival's fighting skills. She could take him.

Chapter Thirteen

For the sake of her job, Chantay just locked Deontay in cold storage until the police showed up. While she and Snap wrestled to get Deontay into the freezer, Janeen posted the harrowing tale on her Facebook page, complete with a duck-lipped selfie. Chelsea helped herself to a few more pieces of chicken with the side of coleslaw and went to sit in the dining room to eat. A few minutes later, Snap popped in the uncomfortable vinyl booth across from her with his own plate.

"We deserve this for solving the case," he said, smiling and chewing.

"What case? All I did was notice a dirty wall. And all you did was grab a dude and put him in the freezer."

"Yeah, Chels. That's called police work. Only we did it for chicken wings. Say what you want, I'm calling this one The Case of The Greasy Wall."

"What about the Case of the Free Wings?" Chelsea countered.

"Face it, there's a pattern forming."

"What pattern, Snap?"

He calmly looked up from his plate and stared into her eyes. "A pattern of using that brain of yours to help other people. You helped Carter solve a murder. A murder! You just saved somebody's job! This is huge!"

"And I kept Olive out of juvie."

"I still can't believe you barged in that woman's house like that." Snap shook his head.

"Really? Do you know me? Me and you have some epic barge stories."

Snap nodded. "I'm just saying, this could be our thing."

"Our thing?"

"Every famous detective has a sidekick. I got you, Scooby. I'll be your Shaggy," he said.

"I'm not a detective and the only thing you and Shaggy have in common is your weight."

Snap was offended. "Shaggy wish he had my body. Don't make me take my shirt off."

"You always looking for a reason to take your shirt off. I can't take you nowhere," Chelsea said.

Their loud laughter was a surprise to Janeen, who was still shaken by what happened. "Why is they laughing? Ain't nothing funny. We all coulda died."

"Them two always been goofy," Chantay said as she walked from behind the counter with another plate of wings toward the giggling pair. She dropped the plate in front of Snap. "Thanks yaw for helping me keep my job."

Snap looked at Chelsea, who was chewing her food and ignoring Chantay. "Chelsea? Do you have anything to say?"

"Thank you for saving me from the hot grease," Chelsea said without emotion.

Chantay nodded and turned to walk away.

"Yaw can do better than that!" Snap said authoritatively. "The Case of the Thieving Fry Cook needs a happy ending."

Chantay turned back and Chelsea took a good look at her longtime nemesis. She was still a pretty girl. She'd traded in her J. Lo-inspired weave for a dreadlocks weave style. It became her. Chelsea wasn't about to say it though.

"When are you due?" Chantay said tightly.

"October."

"The first one is the worst. Take them breathing classes, it'll help with the pain."

"Thanks, Tay."

"And if you get some craving for chicken, we'll take care of you." She smiled. Not a warm smile, kind of forced, in fact. "You too, Snap."

She walked back into the kitchen.

"You happy?" Chelsea asked. "'Cause you being way more Freddy than Shaggy right now."

"The Case of Chicken Shack Thief," he said, laughing.

"The case of we wouldn't even have been here if you wasn't trying to get on that Insta-Rat with the crazy lashes."

"The case of for somebody that needs a fake fiancé you sho is being difficult."

Chelsea laughed so loudly that Chantay and Janeen both jumped. Only Snap could make her laugh like that. The two old friends sat in the uncomfortable vinyl booth eating chicken and teasing each other as if they were in a world all their own.

"I told you, they always been goofy," Chantay reiterated to Janeen, who was in the process of deleting Snap's contact information out of her phone.

"He cute but, I'm straight on him." Janeen rolled her eyes, caught a glimpse of her reflection and decided to take another selfie.

"Snap got it going on. Good job, nice car. But honestly, I don't think nobody can compete with Chelsea," Chantay said before looking back at the freezer door.

"This is false imprisonment!" Deontay was screaming through the freezer door.

"Shut up, thief!" Janeen and Chantay hollered in unison.

Chapter Fourteen

Barristers Ball, April 2015.

Once a year, the who's who of Detroit—from the family Ford to the family Ilitch, the board members from every major corporation, every lawyer with a valid bar number, a host of past and present judges, clerks and assistants, and any police officer that could get the night off and owned a decent suit—dress to impress and come to network and show off. Some said it should be called the Braggart's Ball instead, as most conversations were usually about the spending habits of the prestigious main line.

It was an expensive night of mink coats, luxury vehicles and champagne cocktails with Detroit's elite. Carter French had switched shifts with Woo to get the night off, which meant he would be doing crowd control at the Chris Brown concert, but it was worth it. He had the night off and a millionairess stepmother to purchase a tuxedo for him. What better way to get promoted to detective than by spending an evening hobnobbing with the likes of Detroit prosecutor Kym Worthy and Police Chief Craig? And he had the perfect date in his beautiful baby sister, Chelsea.

She wasn't his first choice. He had been hopeful of taking Benét, his friend with benefits of the last two weeks. That was, until she called him from jail asking for assistance after being arrested on bunco charges. He'd thought she was a kindergarten teacher, not an identity thief. He had to cut her quick, which had left him without a date for the biggest social event of his career. If he couldn't show up with a beautiful woman that adored him, he'd do the next best thing and show up with a beautiful woman that loved him like a brother.

Getting Chelsea, who saw no value in those types of events, to agree to go was not easy. He had to promise her a couture dress, shoes, accessories, hair, makeup and a hundred dollars in cash. Chelsea wouldn't take any of Maddy's money but she had no problem asking Carter for the money that he took.

"Miss Madeleine will set up your accounts if you just ask."

Chelsea's response was always the same. "I don't want her money! I want yours!"

But it was worth it. Chelsea was a vision of loveliness. A black butterfly. She had found a red gown that perfectly fit her hourglass figure and had piled her long, bushy hair into an alluring up-do. She was like a black Eliza Doolittle, being whispered about by every man in the room. Chelsea was so beautiful that when Adrian Gonzalez saw her at the ball, he forgot to make fun of Carter for wearing Tom Ford sunglasses, indoors, after dark, to a black-tie affair. And that was something he wouldn't typically overlook. Laughing at Carter was a sport for him. They weren't exactly friends; they were work rivals who tolerated each other. But Adrian put it all to the side when he saw Chelsea. He asked her to dance and gazed at her infatuatedly for the duration of the song. He would spend weeks calling her, and going into Farmer Roger's to run into her accidentally on purpose before she would agree to go out with him.

But that date didn't end well.

Adrian had managed to avoid Chelsea after that. Partly because he stopped going to Farmer Roger's accidentally on purpose. Mostly because he wasn't friends with Carter. They rarely saw each other outside of work.

Until one sunny afternoon two years later, when he and his partner Woo were called to Big Jack's Chicken Shack. The manager had locked a man in the freezer who was stuttering through his frosted face, something about suing for unlawful imprisonment. Adrian and Woo had a difficult time understanding the sequence of events. She said he stole money from her purse. He said she assaulted him. And the only person that could adequately explain about the hot wall wasn't even an employee. The manager redirected the detectives to a lady in the dining area described as "the pregnant greedy chick on her third plate of free wings". The whole situation sounded screwy, so they approached the table cautiously, hands on weapons but not drawn.

Woo took the lead. "Ma'am, we need to ask you some questions." He stopped when he saw her face. "Look, A! It's Chels! Why am I not surprised? " Looking back at Chantay, he said, "Bring me a plate of them wings, girl." And he sat next to her.

Adrian sat next to Snap with far less enthusiasm. "Hello, Chelsea French."

"Sup, A. How you been?"

"Quite well, thank you," he said, still carrying the tension of their last meeting.

Woo cut in, all smiles. "Wait till we tell Carter we saw you!"

"Don't leave out the name of the manager. That's the best part," Snap said. Chelsea chuckled.

Chapter Fifteen

Three hours later, Carter sat in his favorite watering hole, The Mixx, a frequent cop hangout, drinking with his new partner, Totty Bester, whom he'd only been assigned to for about a week. She thought it would be good to grab a beer and get to know each other.

Totty was a well-seasoned detective and Carter was still new to the game. Carter admired her confidence and comfort playing in a man's game, although he knew better than to say that to her.

He expected to learn a few things about police politics from Totty. Her name had been linked to at least two affairs with previous police bigwigs. It took a certain kind of woman to keep her job after being named co-respondent in a public divorce. The press had nicknamed her Totty the Hottie because she was, well, a hottie. She'd gone viral when a friend of a suspect posted a pic of her making an arrest. She was bending over and the friend had caught a good angle of her voluptuous hips and thighs. He hashtagged it #PigBae and it went around the world. For a while after that, the other ladies in the precinct blatantly copied her style all the way down to her cranberry hair streaks.

Carter was waiting for the right time or the right number of drinks to ask her about the nickname, the viral pics, and all of her public relations faux pas in general.

"Is that Totty the Hottie over there?" Woo's bellowing voice came from the doorway of the bar. Totty looked up and smiled as the room of cops yelled out, "Woo!"

"Wassup, everybody! Long day at the office?" The room filled with laughter as he crossed to embrace Totty. Woo had the soul of a cop, the personality of a stand-up comedian, and the physical build of an NBA player. He had to lean over to hug Totty, who fell into his embrace like a damsel in distress. He even looked like a ball player, wearing a baseball cap with his suit. All the ladies loved Woo (whose real name was Alan). He knew how to enter a room and command all the attention. So much so that no one ever noticed that Adrian was usually walking in with him.

"Yo, French, we saw your sister today," Woo said, taking a seat at the bar next to Totty.

"Where?"

"A theft at the Chicken Shack." Adrian beckoned the bartender. "Don't worry, she's fine."

"What happened? Is she a witness?" he asked, slightly alarmed.

"No, Carter, she's not a witness." Adrian's tone was condescending. "An employee just stole some money. We were also told to tell you the manager's name is Chantay Leonard."

Carter's face fell hard. It almost cracked. "If Chels and Tay were in the same room and the only law broken was theft, it was a good day." Carter knew that those two were more likely to commit assault with deadly intent. "What was she even doing at the Shack? On Fenkell Avenue? She has no business in that neighborhood in her condition!"

"Hoodrats love chicken," Adrian said. Before Carter could respond to that, Woo interjected.

"She actually solved the case, Car."

"What?" Totty asked in disbelief. "Solved the case? Like Masterpiece Theater?"

Woo nodded. "Basically. She looked at the evidence and named the thief before we even arrived on the scene."

"Before we were even called," Adrian added. "It was like Sherlock Holmes."

Woo and Adrian filled Carter in on what happened as they understood it. Knowing Chelsea's mind and Snap's impetuous savior complex, he was able to follow along. But Totty was confused.

"Uh, Carter, you'd better get your sister before she get herself hurt." Totty had an authoritative tone. "Detroit is not like a TV crime show."

"Maybe Detroit wouldn't be so bad if more citizens like Chelsea took a stand. I think it was cool what she did. But then again, I remember that time she called out the picnic man. Saved me a day of paperwork," Woo said.

"Picnic man?" Totty asked.

"Chels and I were at a picnic and these two guys got into a fight over a woman. She was married to one guy and smashing the other. It was messy. The next day, the one guy comes to the precinct and files a complaint saying that the other guy stole his watch in retaliation. And of course, it wasn't a cheap watch. Guy claims it was a Rolex worth around fifteen hundred," Carter said.

Woo chimed in. "So my gut told me the guy was lying and trying to jam the man up over his wife, but of course I couldn't prove it. Then Chelsea walks into the station!"

"She was investigating the missing watch?" Totty asked.

"No. Nothing like that. She and I had plans for lunch and she was meeting me. So she's sitting out front, waiting for me and recognizes the guy," Carter said.

94

"I'm taking this man's statement and can't help but notice this chick behind him. First she sized him up with her eyes. Then she tilts her head and scrunches her face up. Finally, her eyes got big. I'm thinking somebody crazy done wandered in off the street. But when Carter came out front, she jumped up and whispered something in his ear."

"What did she say?" Totty asked Carter. She was enthralled.

Adrian smacked his lips.

"She noticed he didn't have a tan line on either wrist, but had lines from his T-shirt. The day before had been a scorcher."

"He wasn't wearing a watch. Wow. Sounds like she has good powers of observation."

"No! She just got lucky! What does a ghetto girl like her know about real police work?" Adrian said. "Okay, she's smarter than Carter. But so is a monkey!"

Woo stood up, just in case Carter took a well-deserved swing at Adrian. Everyone in the precinct knew their rivalry was dangerously close to fisticuffs. But Carter just smiled.

"You're just mad she saw through you. Your mistake was underestimating my sister. Saw a girl from Elmirdale that works at Farmer Roger's and thought she was easy pickings. And when she called out all of your bull, you got mad.

Chelsea is more Sherlock than hoodrat. She's a human lie detector and that's kryptonite to a man that lies to every woman he meets."

Woo laughed. He knew his partner inside and out. "Ooohhh, burn."

Carter turned to Totty. "This genius tells her he was almost in the space program."

Totty laughed out. "Come on, A! You out here tellin' chicks you was in NASA?"

"I could've been an astronaut!" Adrian defended.

"Not after Chels rattled off all the requirements. She told him that his glasses were too thick. He needs 20/200 vision and Adrian is nearsighted."

Woo howled with laughter. "Should've worn your contacts!"

Carter continued. "He told her he played ball in college, was pre-med, and had been sending money to a family in Zimbabwe. Chelsea caught every lie and at the end of the night he dropped her off and didn't even wait for her to get to the door."

Woo and Totty laughed uncontrollably as his hand was slapping the bar.

"Yeah, well, you still wore sunglasses to the Barristers Ball," was Adrian's only quip.

"I can't wait to meet your sister now. She's amazing," Totty said, breathing heavy from laughing and needing a sip of water.

Carter nodded. "She's something."

As if a light-bulb had gone off over his head, Woo exclaimed, "Maybe Shorty should be a detective!"

Carter scoffed. "It's not safe. Besides, she's pregnant."

"Exactly. By a thug in jail for murder. And that's not hoodrat-ish at all." Adrian made one last sarcastic crack before dropping a twenty dollar bill on the bar and walking out.

Woo stood up. "I guess we're out." He kissed Totty on the forehead. "Call me later, beautiful. And Carter, I don't care what A says, your sister is cool with me." He dapped up a few more people before walking out the bar.

Carter looked at Totty, who was still blushing. "You and Woo, huh?"

"Maybe. We'll see."

"He's a good man."

"So are you. And I hear you're rich."

Now Carter was blushing. "I'm not rich."

"About your sister. I would hate to see her get hurt. She could get a private investigator's license. Maybe catch cheating husbands or insurance fraud. No danger."

Carter shook his head. "My little sister has all the ability but not an ounce of ambition. She's the most uninspired person I know. And she'll never change."

"At least she can be useful to you if ever you need it."

Carter thought back to that time in the restaurant when she was useful on his first case. Then the last time he went to visit his sister and she flat-out refused to help him. He wondered how much longer she would freeze him out.

"Enough about Chelsea. I have a question for you."

"Shoot."

"Did you really have an affair with Benny Napoleon?"

Totty rolled her eyes. "If we're gonna get into this, we'll need another round."

Chapter Sixteen

There is a misconception that hood folk don't have nice things. They do, they just move them into their houses in the middle of the night so that the hoods in the hood won't get any ideas. Between Snap's reputation and his closeness to Carter, most people on the block knew better than to even attempt to upset his peace of mind. Still, he kept the outside of his house modest, parked his Escalade in the garage every night, and tried not to floss his massive gym shoe collection too hard when he was on the block.

One of the benefits of Chelsea and Snap's lifestyle of living in the homes left by their parents was having the disposable income to justify extravagant purchases. Where Chelsea had a weakness for things cushy and soft, like body contouring mattress sets and Egyptian thread counts, Snap, in typical male fashion, had four flat-screen televisions.

He had a seventy inch in his basement, complete with theater seats he had installed after one of his profit-sharing checks. It was for movie nights and March Madness. He had a twenty-four inch, voice activated model mounted to the wall of his kitchen that his dates usually found impressive when he was coercing them into cooking. He had a forty-six inch that sat on the dresser in his bedroom and a fifty-five inch on a stand in his living room, also known as the dance floor room.

When Snap was growing up, his mother, Jackie, would slap him upside the head every time she caught him playing in her museum of a living room. She had a couch that had maybe been sat on five times. It wasn't covered in plastic because as she used to say, "I'm not protecting my furniture from kids. These kids better do what the hell I say." And that meant staying out of her living room.

After twenty-three years of maintaining a relationship with Snap's mother on one side of town, Snap's father, T.C. Haines, finally divorced his wife on the other side of town and married Jackie. When Jackie moved out, she took her pristine couch and coffee table set with her, leaving a huge space in the living room. Snap, the new man of the house, opted to put one of his giant TVs against the wall. And that's all. When Carter had helped him move the TV in, he'd looked around the empty room. "Why do you need a dance floor?"

"Because I like to dance," he answered. The dance floor room had been host to many of Snap's parties over the years. Jackie was appalled every time she came to visit her only son. For a while, she would try to clean up after him and scolded his bachelor ways. But once she found a used condom in the kitchen, she stopped visiting. Now if Snap wanted to see his mother, he had to go all the way to Clinton Township.

Lately, Snap and Chelsea had been watching old music videos on YouTube and reenacting the choreography. They took turns picking the artists and had worked their way through the Janet Jackson, Aaliyah, Dru Hill and Usher playlists. If there was no dance routine actually in the video, they would just do whatever dances were popular at the time. It was their thing. It was relaxing and nostalgic. Snap thought they could use a little of that after the day they had.

"It's barely nine-thirty. Stop being a granny. Let's dance off all that chicken," he said to Chelsea as he pulled into his driveway.

"Babe's sleepy." Chelsea blamed her growing fetus for everything she didn't want to do.

"Babe just needs to move," he said, dismissing her. Twenty minutes later, he had Chelsea dragged into his house with his YouTube queued up to "Drop it Like It's Hot."
"Let's do the old talent show routine," Snap said excitedly.

In tenth grade, Snap, Chelsea and an upperclassman had put a routine together that they were sure would win the Mackenzie High School talent show. And when the music began to play, all the feelings of that day returned to Chelsea. The excitement, the angst, and the annoyance of losing to Whitney Barron all came back like it was yesterday. Before she knew it she was up on her feet doing the steps.

"We should've won this one," Chelsea said in mid-crip walk.

When Snap was on the dance floor, all of his friends knew not to disturb him. So when Carter looked through the window and saw him and Chels dancing, he did what everyone did. He walked in and joined them.

"As I recall, when Whitney and her dance team jumped up in matching outfits to Disco Inferno, it was a wrap. Whole school loved them. 50 Cent was hot back then."

Carter was that upperclassman.

"Oh, really?" Chelsea started. "As I recall you were offbeat." The three finished the routine all the way to the last falsetto Snoop-- before speaking.

"I think I've gotten better," Carter said, panting.

Snap hugged his old friend whom he hadn't seen since things had gotten weird between him and Chelsea.

"Car! Where you been, bro?"

"I know, man. I've just been busy with this new job lately. Trying to prove myself."

Chelsea thought to herself, Carter's need to prove himself had landed James in jail.

As if he knew what she was thinking, Snap addressed the situation. "Listen, you two. This beef ain't working for me. Yaw are my best friends. We can't do this."

Chelsea and Carter, matched in their faces of shame, both dropped their heads.

"Chelsea, I'm really sorry."

"Don't apologize to me, Car! Apologize to Babe for putting his father in jail!"

Carter went to defend his actions but got lost in the word 'his'. He smiled, broad and proud. "His?"

"Is this the gender reveal?" Snap said.

Chelsea shrugged. "I guess."

"You hear that, Snap? We're having a boy!" Carter hugged his sister and kissed her forehead. "There's nothing I won't do for him, Chelsea. He isn't just yours. He's ours."

"All of ours," Snap said, joining the hug.

Chelsea, smothered by her two tall protectors, had never felt more loved. She embraced them both and knew her babe would always be cared for…even if James never came home.

"I heard about what happened today," Carter said, breaking the hug chain. "Kind of reckless."

"You mad?" Chelsea asked.

"No. Anything that shows up Adrian Gonzalez is all right with me. But maybe next time, don't confront a thief."

"There won't be a next time. Snap just didn't want to see crazy Tay lose her job."

"How is Tay looking these days?" Carter asked sheepishly.

"Still fine," Snap said. "She got that earthy Jill Scott thing going on. More attitude though. I can't lie, when she snatched ole boy down off that fence, it was kinda hot."

Chelsea smacked her lips. "It was not hot. It was ratchet."

Carter gave Snap a look that said, Look who's talking? but he didn't say it out loud. Chelsea was in denial about her own ratchet fighting habits.

Snap picked up his remote control to advance to the next song on the playlist. It was Yeah by Usher, featuring Lil Jon and Ludacris. "This used to be my jam!" He hit play and as the intro dropped, he began to mimic Usher's robotic dance moves to perfection. "Aye! I think Chels should open her own detective joint and start helping people." He immediately turned up the volume to drown out the inevitable sounds of Carter's criticism.

"Absolutely not!" Carter was saying, but Snap couldn't hear him. He just turned the volume on his sub-woofers up a little bit more and sang along with the song.

He was in his zone, dancing and happy. He looked over at Chelsea, who was shaking her head and lip-syncing No instead of "Yeah". He grabbed her.

"Shut up and dance, Scooby!"

She laughed and fell into choreographic formation. As the two bopped along with Usher, Carter leaned against the same wall Jackie used to scold him for touching. He watched them dance, and a deep sinking feeling hit him in the pit of his stomach. He knew he wouldn't be able to stop them.

But for the next three months, Carter didn't hear a peep about Chelsea solving any more crimes. Everyone returned to their normal monotony. Carter continued his training as a police detective. Snap worked tirelessly at building cars for the world to drive. Chelsea spent her second trimester preparing for her baby. And the distance between Chelsea and James grew as quickly as her belly.

Then as summer ended it became clear that the murder of Boudreau Fontaine was not settled. The streets still had a verdict to render. And the jury was deliberating.

Chapter Seventeen

Romeo Qadir had only been out of law school five years and already he was named in The Michigan Chronicle's Most Prominent 30 Under 30. At 29, he was fighting city council, protesting water shut-offs, threatening slumlords and defending indigent clients against a variety of crimes out of the public defender's office. He hated when people referred to him as 'woke'. 'Woke' implied that someone was first sleeping, but Romeo was born into this. His parents were both raised in New York and came from two different struggles. His mother, Rashidah, was from a family of Black Nationalists, mostly Nation of Islam. His father, Samir, was born in Tehran before the overthrow of the Pahlavi dynasty, in which his family had actively participated. The two had met at a protest against discrimination as students at Columbia University. Matched in their revolutionary spirits, they set aside their cultural differences, fell in love, married and moved to Detroit for teaching opportunities at Wayne State University. She taught African-American Studies, and he taught International Economics. They had also published a book (about improving Middle Eastern and African-American relations) that was required reading in three colleges. The Qadirs were the walking woke.

They had raised Romeo and his sister Audre to be free thinkers committed to helping their fellow man and fighting oppression. Audre had founded a women's organization called The Lorde's Work. Romeo was a lawyer and advocate for those that most needed him. And he was Carter's friend.

Romeo's Afro-Persian features gave him a racially ambiguous look. Tall, slim and very fair, he could pass for Black or Middle Eastern, sometimes even be mistaken for Latino. But today he looked like trouble in a navy blue and white snapback with the word Tehran printed in bold and pulled down over his light brown eyes and a Detroit vs. Everybody hoodie zipped over a Detroit Tigers T-shirt. Romeo never left home without the rebellion. He was a proud Persian, uplifting his city and supporting the home team all in one outfit. Go Tigers!

He sat across the table from Carter, having lunch at Lafayette Coney Island just a short walk from Comerica Park where the two were headed for an afternoon baseball game. Carter wondered who had given Ro the expensive hoodie. He knew Ro would never spend $50 on anything. When it came to clothes, the two friends were 180 degrees apart. Where Carter was couture, Romeo was thrift.

Carter had started his day shopping for the game. First, he'd picked up a pair of Kameko's customized Air Jordan's, which had cost him $1,000 because of the rush job. They turned out perfectly and matched the same hues of orange and blue on the T-shirt that Koolade Temple, his streetwear stylist, had selected for him at the AYV Midtown store.

Carter had changed his clothes there. He didn't mind dressing in team colors as long as he could do it with style. And the store was just minutes from Lafayette Coney Island.

Romeo, who had probably only put 15 seconds of thought into his outfit that morning, hated to see Carter waste money on clothes. "People are starving, man," he would always say. He was frugal. He didn't even have cable. But it never stopped the ladies from loving Romeo. He'd start talking about mentoring kids or Project Innocence, and the women would just swoon.

Including Chelsea and Diane.

Carter had met Romeo when he was fresh out of law school. Carter had to testify for the very first time against a man he had arrested. Diane had mandated the entire family come to court for support. Carter tried to deter them from coming, but his mother had her mind set on seeing her eldest child shine. She even bought Carter a new tie. Young Romeo was representing the defendant and successfully got his client acquitted. Carter took it rather hard, and was surprised when Romeo approached the French family after the trial.

"Excuse me, Officer French. You did great in there. You're a good officer. You can't take these things personally." Romeo was smiling and extending his hand. "No hard feelings?"

"No, he's fine," Diane said. "We're his parents, Diane and Ray. And this is his very single sister, Chelsea." She had pulled

Chelsea by the arm and offered her to Romeo like an Incan sacrifice.

"Ma!" Chelsea said in vain; Diane wasn't listening.

"Do you have a girlfriend?" Diane asked an embarrassed Romeo.

"No, ma'am, I'm single. I've only just moved back. I was in law school in D.C."

"Surprised a tall guy like you chose the law over basketball," Ray teased.

"I played ball too, in undergrad. Shooting guard."

Ray smiled. "I was a guard in high school. Did you meet my daughter, Chelsea?"

"I'm never going anywhere with this family again!" Chelsea said.

Carter laughed. "Sorry, Mr. Qadir. You've said two words my parents love: single and basketball."

"Call me Romeo." He smiled and looked at Chelsea. Her legs buckled.

"Baby girl, it's not every day you meet a single, handsome lawyer," Diane whispered in Chelsea's ear so loudly everyone heard her. "Invite him to dinner."

"You just did," Chelsea said at a normal volume.

"I'd love to come for dinner, Mrs. French."

So, Romeo came over for dinner and after the meal, all the young people, including Snap (who had invited himself when he smelled Diane's pot roast), sat on the back porch and ate peach cobbler. The guys talked about basketball, and Chelsea pretended to understand. Later, Diane had sent Carter and Snap to take out garbage bags so that Romeo could be alone with Chelsea long enough to ask her on a proper date. Diane had been dropping hints all night.

Five years later, the fling with Chelsea was a bust and Diane had passed away, but Romeo and Carter were still homies. They went to as many games as their schedules allowed, they would always go tomcatting after either had a breakup, and whenever Carter had a real problem, he'd call Romeo.

He had just spent an entire meal catching Romeo up on James's conviction.

"And ever since he went to jail, she's been different," Carter said, referring to Chelsea.

"What do you mean, different?"

"I don't know. But she solved a murder."

Romeo's eyes got big, his face relaxed into a smile, and then he laughed. "I could see that."

"You're not surprised?" Carter asked.

"Nah, Bro. Chelsea's brain is kind of phenomenal. I've seen it in action."

"When?"

"Well," Romeo began, "there was this one time that I had to cancel a date with her because I had received some new evidence for one of my cases. Chelsea was disappointed because I was supposed to be taking her to see Janelle Monae. But I had to work, right? She asked if we could meet at my office that afternoon. I won't lie to you, Car, I was hoping for sex. But instead, she shows up and asks me all about my case. I didn't give her any names, but I told her the crux of what my client was accused of. The new evidence was a witness statement. A neighbor claimed to have seen my client committing the crime. I didn't tell her anything that would violate my ethics. But I did read her the statement."

"Let me guess, she found the lie?" Carter asked.

"Dude!" Romeo exclaimed. "She did this weird head tilt thing. Then pieced together a compelling theory of the crime, and we still made the concert. That was the first and only time she spent the night with me."

Carter growled.

"I know, I know that's your sister. Nothing graphic. I'm just saying, it took our relationship to the next level. I woke up in love with her. I wanted her to be my assistant, maybe go to paralegal school so we could open an office together. I had all these plans for us. But when she woke up..." Romeo recalled.

"She blew it all off and then went to the grocery store."

Carter knew his sister's routine like the back of his hand.

"And she was probably running late."

Romeo nodded. "We broke up a week later. And I couldn't listen to Janelle Monae anymore."

"I can't believe you never told me this," Carter said.

"I didn't want you to think I was shallow. Because I'm not. But I have big plans, and I don't know what to do with an underachiever." Romeo seemed heartfelt. "And I didn't want to say anything bad about your sister."

Carter understood. Romeo had made a name for himself in local politics in the last five years. He was a Top 30 under 30, a

Detroit Who's Who, and one of the most eligible bachelors in Michigan. He wouldn't settle for a store clerk.

"So anyway, yeah, I'm not surprised she solved a murder. When she's motivated, she's a great detective," Romeo said.

"Now Snap is encouraging her to use her 'gift' to help people."

"We should all be using our gifts to help people, Car," the altruistic Romeo said. "What's the big deal?"

Carter's face was somber. "I'm concerned that my baby sister could get hurt. These streets are crazy, not to mention the Fontaines want revenge for what happened to Bou."

Romeo had once represented Boudreau Fontaine against a breaking and entering charge. He knew just how violently savage that family was. The father, Arcangelo, had threatened Romeo if he didn't get Bou's charges dropped. Romeo had politely explained to Mr. Fontaine that Iranians were not known for peaceful resolutions. His exact words were: "Something happens to me, and you'll have to explain it to the Persian Mafia." That seemed to be enough to subdue Arcangelo. Romeo had no further issues after that.

"We picked up a crackhead two weeks ago. He offered to snitch. He heard Marin Fontaine, the oldest brother, saying he would take his revenge by making his brother's killer feel his pain."

"Maybe he was just trying to stay out of the county jail," Romeo offered.

"Maybe. Or maybe he heard Marin make a real threat against James's family. James has a sister. And a mother. And very soon, a son. Chelsea needs to get out that neighborhood and sit her ass down somewhere safe."

"Look, we'll get to the bottom of this. The Fontaines would be insane to mess with a cop's sister. Chelsea will be alright."

Carter nodded.

Romeo checked his watch. "Hey, it's time to go. We could both use a beer."

The two friends walked across the street and up to Comerica Park. Carter's badge got them through the slowest parts of the lines as thousands of Detroiters piled in to see the Detroit Tigers play the Oakland A's. Once they got up to the VIP gate, Romeo pulled the tickets out of his pocket. A colleague was letting him use his suite. "Is your partner still coming?" he asked Carter.

Carter looked out and spotted Totty decked in very casual wear bouncing up the stairs. "Here she comes." Carter, Romeo and every other man within the sight radius of Totty's gait stared at her ample and revealed thighs and cleavage scantily covered by Tigers apparel. "What do you think?" Carter asked his wingman.

"I approve."

Totty reached the top steps smiling. "Carter! Let's get drunk! Who's your friend?"

Chapter Eighteen

"What we gon' do for Chelsea?" Miss Madeleine asked her daughters, Diamondique and Sapphire Baker, while they sat waiting for the Annual Miami Fashion Walk to begin.

Diamondique had considered herself a fashionista long before the money came. And now that she had it, she wouldn't miss events like these. She folded up her program and looked at her mother.

"As far as?"

"A baby shower. Should we just rent out a banquet hall or something?"

"Ma, I don't think Chelsea would want all that fuss. You know how she is. Just send her a nursery and a nanny. Call it a day." It wasn't that Diamondique didn't like Chelsea. But everyone knew Chelsea didn't like Madeleine.

"She's so weird. I don't want to waste my time, but her father expects me to do something. And I expect her to be uncooperative. She always is."

"Maybe she could just come down here, stay in Boca, and we can do a cookout on the beach. Invite all the family," Sapphire, the youngest daughter, suggested.

"After she blew us off on Mother's Day?" Diamondique said, referencing Chelsea's no-show the last time the family had come together. "So we go through all the trouble to throw her a baby shower and then she don't even get on the plane?"

The Baker women were still perturbed that Chelsea had ignored her invitation on Mother's Day. She was too good to give Miss Madeleine her due. Even Carter took time from his demanding police job to fly down for the weekend. He brought a gift for his stepmother (that his stepmother had probably paid for), but still. Carter got an A for effort, while spoiled Chelsea stayed home and pouted. A month later she begged her father to return to Detroit for Father's Day. Of course, he went.

Sapphire disagreed. "Mother's Day is a hard time for people that lost their real moms. And you know Chelsea and her mother were very close. Maybe it would be sad for her to watch us with you."

"I did notice Carter getting a little gloomy. He misses her too. He still showed up. But he got more sense than Chelsea. That's why he's so successful, and she's just..." Madeleine began.

Sapphire cut her off. "Exactly what you were before you won the lottery?"

Madeleine rolled her eyes hard at her youngest daughter. Sapphire was always taking Chelsea's side no matter how horribly she behaved. It was infuriating. Sapphire seemed to be the only one sympathetic to Chelsea and Carter losing their mother to cancer and then their father to Madeleine in the same year. Because once the money came, Ray and Madeleine left Detroit for coastal waters and sunnier days. Carter just handled it better than Chelsea.

"Don't yaw two start!" Diamondique scolded. "This ain't the place for all that. We supposed to be classy! Look, Ma's right. Ray wants something nice for his only daughter. We gotta do something. And since she likes you the most Sapph, you gotta get her down here. Me and Ma will do the rest. Now shut up, the show is starting." Diamondique was the oldest and the child of Madeleine's youth. She had been refereeing her mother and younger siblings her whole life.

As the voice of the Emcee came above the loud music blaring from the speakers, the audience began to clap in excitement and Sapphire could only shake her head hopelessly. Getting Chelsea out of Detroit was going to be a challenge. It would take a series of lies for sure. But how do you lie to Chelsea?

Chapter Nineteen

"What's wrong with my car?" A perplexed Kevin asked his girlfriend, Olive, while hitting the hood of his brand new very used 2008 Chevy Silverado that his father had gotten him for his 17th birthday. "All we need is some gas money, and we're good to go."

Olive smacked her lips. "This is the senior summer picnic, Kevin! You're about to be a senior. You have to floss. And we can't floss in this old truck."

"Why you gotta hate on my truck? I been picking you up every day since I got this baby. It's better than the bus." Kevin's feelings were hurt.

This was Olive's first year going to the Senior Picnic. You had to either be a senior or dating one if you wanted the coveted secret invite. And she wanted to make a splash. It was never too early for Kevin to start campaigning for Homecoming King and Queen.

"Look Kev, my cousin Carter got a Audi almost as lit as Tony Stark's. It wouldn't hurt just to ask him if we could borrow it for the day. You're a good driver. He'll say yes. Trust me."

Olive pulled out her new iPhone, the one Uncle Ray had bought her for Easter after she'd said she was too old for a new dress and hat.

She sent a text. *Hey Car. How's your day going? Fighting crime?*

He responded right away. *No. I'm at a baseball game. What's up Ollie? You need some money?*

Olive: *No, I'm straight. I do need another favor tho.*

Carter: *Anything Baby Cuz.*

Olive: *Can I borrow the Audi for the senior picnic in 2 weeks? Kevin is a great driver. No accidents or tickets.*

Carter: *He's only been driving a month. I thought he had a car?*

Olive: *It's lame.*

Carter: *I don't know Ollie. When?*

Olive: *2 weeks from Wednesday.*

Carter: *I work during the week. I don't get home until after 6.*

Olive: *Cool! Picnic doesn't start until 10!*

Carter: *NO.*

Olive: *Pleaseeeeeeeeeee!*

Carter: *Hell NO. But you funny.*

Kevin was looking over Olive's shoulder and read Carter's response. "Well, that's that."

But Olive wasn't ready to concede defeat that fast. "I wonder, would Chelsea even notice if her car wasn't in the garage?"

"Ummm! Bad idea!" His face became panic-stricken. "We are not taking Chelsea's car without her permission. That's grand theft auto. I should know. I have the game! And Carter will arrest us for sure."

"He would never. Most that would happen is she would be mad. It's not like she even care about that car. She'll get over it."

"Leave me out of it," Kevin protested.

"No. I need you to distract her while I get the keys out of her drawer. We'll have the car back before she even notices it's gone."

"What's wrong with the women in your family? You're all insane!" Kevin said in frustration.

First, Chelsea had burst in on him and his mother at their home, then great Aunt Grace had tried to sneak and cut

Kevin's hair one day when he'd dozed off on her couch. Now Olive was plotting a car theft and had made him both the distraction and the getaway driver. She didn't even have a license.

Olive smiled. "It must be this Superwoman DNA."

"More like super crazy woman DNA!" Kevin said, knowing he had been overruled again by his girlfriend. Olive always got her way. "I better not end up in a boy's home!"

Olive stepped closer to him and kissed him on the mouth. His arms relaxed and wrapped around her waist. She held the back of his neck with one hand and placed her other arm on his shoulder.

"If you help me, I promise to give you this and more."

Kevin, drenched in hormones and teenage libido, nodded his head in devotion.

Chapter Twenty

Whenever Snap and Chelsea, who both worked irregular schedules that could change in a moment, both had a day off, it became their Sunday.

The last couple of weeks, it had been a Wednesday. So Wednesday became Sunday, and like many people, they had a habit of enjoying a big Sunday breakfast. Snap would drive up to Eagle Coney Island on Plymouth Road and order a bacon and cheese omelet for himself with a side of hash browns and wheat toast. For Chelsea, a veggie omelet with a side of bacon, a side of sausage, and in the months since Babe had invaded her body, an additional side of pancakes. Snap would usually bring the carryout breakfast orders to Chelsea's house where they would spend the day getting caught up on DVR recordings of their favorite TV shows.

But not this particular Wednesday. While turning into his driveway with the warm breakfasts securely strapped into his passenger side by a seatbelt, he recognized the ostentatious ruby red convertible Bentley coupe in Chelsea's driveway.

Her stepbrother Rashad was visiting.

Chelsea opened the front door and gave Snap a look that verified what he already believed to be true. Rashad's visit was unexpected.

"What's up, Snap?" Rashad jumped up off the couch to greet him. "Let me help you with the bags."

"Sup, Fam? If I had known you was coming, I'da grabbed you breakfast."

"It's cool. My nutritionist got me eating real healthy," Rashad paused. "I got a nutritionist now. I decided it was time to get my life together. She made me a smoothie for breakfast."

"That's wassup," Chelsea said, not letting Rashad's new healthy lifestyle stop her from enjoying her deliciously fattening fare. She was tearing open the bags and shoveling the large, greasy portions onto her plate.

"Chelsea, I was hoping I could talk you into taking a ride with me today."

"Where to? I need to get caught up on How To Get Away With Murder."

"Just a short errand. I got a business meeting."

"What kind of business, Shad?"

"Well," he began, "I'm gon' buy a studio. 6 Million Ways Inc. Yaw heard of them, right?"

"Yeah. They got that rapper, Magnif. He's cold. I bump his mixtape," Snap said.

"I like the song about the girl taking revenge on her ex. What's her name?" Chelsea asked, cutting her pancakes.

"Belly-Belly," Rashad said with a smile. "That's my girl."

"She is fine as hell. She gon' be at this meeting? I'ma need to change my shirt." Snap glanced down at the stains on the shirt he had slept in.

"Who said you were invited?" Chelsea teased Snap. She would never deny him an opportunity to spit game to a beautiful woman. She turned her attention back to Rashad.

"So, are you buying the building and the equipment?"

"All of it. The artists too. I'm finna be a mogul," Rashad said proudly.

The room got eerily quiet as Snap and Chelsea looked at one another and then immediately back at their food.

"I was kicking it with Birdman and Mannie Fresh in Miami a couple of weeks ago. You know, poppin' bottles and talking about money," Rashad started, but Snap cut him off.

"Birdman? From Cash Money?"

"Yeah, that's the kind of circles I'm running in now, Snap. You know how embarrassing it is to be at a table full of ballers and be the only one that don't have a label?"

"Do Maddy know?" Chels asked, still looking down. She was afraid if she looked up and caught eye contact with Snap, they'd both burst out laughing.

"You know my momma's a hater. She be trying to cut me off. I'm like, how you gon' cut me off when I'm the one that went to the liquor store and played your numbers for you that day?"

"Cut you off?" It had never occurred to Chelsea that Maddy had an off switch for her favorite child. "You musta did something real crazy."

Rashad smacked his lips. This was usually an indication that he was going to tell a story in such a way that he was without blame.

"You know Sapphire like keeping kids, right? So instead of her renting that space on Davidson for her little daycare, I decided to buy her a building on Ewald Circle. It used to be a church, so I figured it was legit. Long story short, the building had asbestos, and Sapphire got sued. And Momma was all like, 'I gotta pay all this money. It's on you.' But why would I think a Deacon would sell me a dirty building?"

"You didn't get an inspection before you bought it?" Snap asked, already knowing the answer.

"Come on, Snap! He a man of the Lord," Rashad replied.

"I'd cut you off too," were Chelsea's only words - a similar sentiment to what she'd said when it had all gone down.

"That's why I need you to go with me to this meeting. Before I hand this man all this bread, I need you to look him over and tell me if he legit."

When Rashad didn't think, he bought old asbestos buildings and turned them into daycare centers. When he DID think, he came to Chelsea instead of a certified realtor.

"Don't you need a professional for this, Shad?" she asked.

"Of course I'ma get a lawyer to go over the artist's contracts. But I need you at this meeting."

Snap knew Chelsea had a different relationship with Madeleine's offspring. The oldest daughter, Diamondique, used to do her hair when she was in high school, long before Ray and Maddy started messing around. She had a booth set up at the Mammoth Swap Meet on the corner of Grand River and Greenfield, where all the high school girls used to line up every weekend for her $25 flat iron special. She never got her cosmetology license, but she was good at getting hair straight.

And she was also selling knock-off designer purses at the time. She could make a sixteen-year-old feel like a celebrity.

The youngest daughter, Sapphire, was as soft-spoken and mild-tempered as Maddy was loud and abrasive. Being born last into a house filled with the thundering voices of many women, Sapphire had her spirit crushed pretty much out of the womb. Between Diamondique, her oldest sibling by 20 years, Maddy, Grandmother Poochie, and Aunt Crystal, poor little Sapph was often drowned out. She was always agreeable and easy to love. And the money hadn't changed her. She did love her daycare centers. And she'd still spend the weekends with Chelsea and sleep on her couch when she just wanted to hang out.

But Rashad had hit Chelsea's well-hidden soft spot.

On the day of Ray and Maddy's wedding, just three months after Diane's passing and two weeks before Maddy would become a woman of wealth and leisure, Carter had been dropped off at the house. He needed a ride to the wedding. Money was very much an object in those days, and Carter was living well above his means trying to maintain that suburban apartment. His car needed repairs and when he had to decide between a new suit for the wedding or getting his tire rods replaced, he'd chosen to hitch rides until his next paycheck.

At that point, both Carter and Chelsea were equally incensed with the situation. Their mother was barely cold when Ray

French had not only announced that he was getting married but that it was to Chelsea's store manager.

Chelsea dragged her feet getting dressed for the wedding. She kept saying that she didn't care if they were late. When they finally got into her 2007 Dodge Caliber, she fussed the entire ride, even threatening to tell Maddy what she thought of her. By the time she pulled into the parking lot of the wedding chapel, she was worked into such a frenzy that she whipped the car into the first available parking space, jumped out, and rushed toward the building ready to curse out the whole wedding party, Bishop included.

Rashad met her outside the door all smiles. Chelsea stopped cold in her tracks. He wore a grin brighter than his red bowtie and cummerbund. He hugged Chelsea and then Carter. He went on and on about how happy he was to have a dad and a brother finally. Rashad was the only one of Maddy's children who'd never known his biological father.

As Chelsea would later explain it to Snap, "The worst day of my life was the best day of his." After that, Chelsea kept her feelings about Ray and Maddy's union tight-lipped. Although, she couldn't help her disgusted facial expressions.
Rashad was annoying, and the money had changed him. There was always one get-richer scheme after another. He was determined to take Maddy's millions and make more. Still, Chelsea was oddly fond of Rashad.

"Can you guarantee Belly-Belly will be there?" Snap teased, knowing they were already going.

"Of course he can. He's a mogul," Chelsea answered.

Rashad's face beamed with pride.

Chapter Twenty-One

Chelsea didn't want to ride with Rashad in his Bentley. Not that it wasn't a beautiful car, it was just that Rashad was wild and womanizing. And Chelsea didn't want to sit on any surface where wild things might have occurred.

"Stop trippin'. I get this car detailed every week," was his response.

She reluctantly got in the car. Snap asked if he could drive. Rashad said no, then proceeded to drive entirely too fast out of Elmirdale, north to the I-96 freeway and east to The W Grand Blvd exit. The houses got bigger as they entered into what was once an affluent community. From Motown legends to Black politicians, this used to be a desirable neighborhood. Now it was riddled with blight, abandoned houses and crackheads. They continued on Grand Blvd. until they crossed Woodward Avenue and took a right down Brush, then a left at Baltimore. On the corner was a grimy old building with a large antenna on the roof. It looked something like an abandoned radio station. Rashad pulled into the parking lot.

It was times like this that Chelsea wished Rashad had a more subtle vehicle. The pretty Bentley might not be there when they came out.

If cars were any indication, there were a lot of people inside the studio. Rashad parked his car horizontally across two spots rather obnoxiously. The gated parking lot was to the left of the building but extended to the back. There were two entrances, one in the front and one in the rear. It took Chelsea a couple of rocking attempts before she was able to swing herself up. By the time she had leveraged her weight and steadied herself out of the car, Snap and Rashad were leaning over the open trunk. Chelsea looked inside and saw Rashad stuffing money into a Gucci backpack.

"What the hell, Rashad? Are you trying to get us killed? You can't carry that kind of cash around a neighborhood like this," Chelsea fussed.

"The man wants cash. I'm giving him cash," Rashad said.

"How much is it?" Snap asked.

"$250,000. What a steal!" Rashad was smiling as he stuffed the last of the banded cash into the bag.

Chelsea looked up at the old and grungy building.

"For this dump? I'm already against this deal."

"Not just the building. I'm getting all the equipment, the music, and the rappers."

"How do you buy rappers?" Snap closed the trunk after Rashad lifted the heavy bag out.

It was obvious that Rashad was getting annoyed with all of Snap's and Chelsea's questions. "The contracts. I'm not a slave owner."

The three walked around to the front entrance. It was an old radio station. Chelsea could see the faint outline of call letters on the door. The place obviously hadn't had any exterior remodeling. She wanted to make a crack about it but decided to wait and save up all of her criticisms for a one-time delivery.

They stepped inside and into what would have been a small lobby area, complete with an empty reception desk. The dusty, shabby lobby connected to a long hallway. At one end closest to the lobby was a closed office door with a mailbox slot carved into it. Farther down the hallway, there was a restroom across from two smaller offices. At the end of what appeared to be a bend in the hall, there was a narrower door, likely a supply closet.

"He knows we're here. I sent him a text. Said he'll be out to get us in a minute."

Standing in an open lobby with a bag full of money was making Chelsea feel very uncomfortable. She should never have agreed to come. She felt like a sitting duck just waiting for a thug to jack them.

"This must be the office side. I want to see the studios," Snap said, walking down the hallway. No sooner had he taken a few steps than the first door opened and a tall white man stepped into the hallway. His gaze swiveled from Snap to Rashad.

"Rashad," the man said as he stepped into the hallway. He was of a medium build, with expensive clothes that seemed to be made for his body. Wearing jeans and a light V-neck sweater, he looked like he belonged in the men's section of a Nordstrom's catalog.

Rashad stepped up eagerly to greet the man. "Mr. Harris! These is my peoples I was telling you about." He pointed to Chelsea and Snap, the latter of whom was already down the hall.

Mr. Harris gave Chelsea a scrutinizing glance. "When you said that you were bringing your team, I assumed that you meant," he paused, "professional people."

Snap was too far away to catch the crack, but Chelsea wasn't.

"No, my team is my family. This is my stepsister, Chelsea. If you can convince her that the deal is legit, you can get what's in this bag," Rashad said, holding up the Gucci bag for Mr. Harris to see.

Mr. Harris offered a placating smile.

"The studio is down here," Snap yelled from the other end of the hallway. "I'm going to find Belly!"

"Well, let's begin our tour with the studios." Mr. Harris beckoned for Chelsea to follow.

He led Rashad and Chelsea down the corridor that opened up to the studios. Snap was already ahead of them. As they got closer, they could hear the boom of bass and percussion. The studio side looked much better than the office side. It was high tech, MacBooks and brightly lit flatscreen monitors flashing sound levels, soundproof walls, and noise-reducing microphones.

There were two adjacent studios, each with large glass windows that allowed people to see from the hallway who was recording. Each studio was presently filled with rappers. Studio A had a girl in the booth, Belly-Belly. Chelsea couldn't hear what she was saying, but from her facial expression, it appeared she was poetic and passionately describing something, probably criminal. A dozen people were standing behind the engineer rocking and dancing to her song. In studio B, there was another rapper, a guy, with a long white T-shirt, five or six gold chains, a blingy watch and a baseball cap. He was equally as passionate and also had several people swaying behind his engineer.

"This looks so lit!" Snap said with excitement. "Everybody's here. Belly-Belly, Magnif, KillerKon, DreyZilla. Is this for a new album?" He directed the last question to Mr. Harris.

Mr. Harris snobbishly rolled his eyes. "How on earth would I know?"

In spite of the strong smell of burning marijuana, Chelsea had to admit that the studios were impressive. State of the art equipment, and what appeared to be productive rappers who came to record every day like it was a real job. Everything she had ever read about famous rappers implied a meticulous work ethic. If Rashad had any chance at making this venture work, he would need rappers that worked hard.

"See, Chels! I told you this is a good look. A solid investment. All I need is for somebody in one of them rooms to make me a hit," Rashad said. "And I'll be good. It's Detroit's time. These guys are the next to blow."

"How exactly will you earn money, Shad? "Chelsea asked.

Mr. Harris answered, "In addition to earning fees for the use of the studio, the studio owner also owns the masters of any works produced in this building. In other words, if they make a hit record, he will get the money."

"And you said you weren't a slave owner?" Chelsea said sarcastically with her eyebrow raised.

Just then, the door to Studio A opened, and a young man popped out.

"What's up, Shad?" he said, slapping Rashad's hand. "Thanks for that case of champagne you sent over. But I try to keep my guy sober when we're working."

"I can dig it. But we got something to celebrate later!" he said, jabbing the man with his elbow. "I'll have a big announcement in about an hour."

The man looked confused as he stepped back into the studio.

"Who was that?" Chelsea asked.

"That's Lee Bee. Magnif's manager. He's a good dude," Rashad replied.

He was certainly a cutie, by Chelsea's estimation. He was tall and slim with dreadlocks that hung all the way to his lower back. He had a Rasta vibe from the neck up. But the rest of him was a D-boy, down to his Timberlands.

Chelsea could tell that Mr. Harris was ready to return to his office.

"How does a guy that obviously doesn't like hip-hop end up running a studio in Detroit?" she asked him directly. He was so obviously unhappy; it begged the question.

"My father owned the building when it was a radio station. When it went out of business, we stumbled into the music industry. All of this was his passion, never mine. And then the rappers came." He answered with the same quiet arrogance that he had worn like a coat since he first stepped out of the office. Mr. Harris set off down the hallway. Rashad and Chelsea followed while Snap decided to stay back to ogle Belly-Belly.

"How did you meet this man?" Chelsea whispered to Rashad.

"I had a party at The Henry. I met him in the hotel bar."

The Henry was a high-end hotel located on the historical Henry Ford estate. It was host to many people in business, including international automakers and guests of The Ford Motor Company. Chelsea knew how Rashad partied. He'd likely entered that bar flashing money and making a pigeon of himself to a guy like Harris. He could sell his father's old building for more than it was worth and be free of his inner-city burden.

She wouldn't be able to talk Rashad out of buying this dump. But maybe she could get the price reduced.

Mr. Harris opened his office door, extended his arm, and waved Chelsea and Rashad inside. There were a few papers on the desk, but mostly trinkets. Golf trinkets. A figurine of a man swinging a golf club, a tiny silver-plated bag of golf clubs, and a golf ball perched on a tee in a clear box. There were plaques on the walls for all the times Mr. Harris had placed second or third in a tournament, his set of golf clubs in the corner of the room, and an indoor putting green on the side of his desk closest to the window that faced the parking lot.

It was safe to assume what he enjoyed doing in his spare time.

Chelsea was at the stage in her pregnancy where she was getting weird leg cramps for no reason. The only thing that seemed to help was walking the cramps away. So she didn't want to sit in the chair that Mr. Harris had pulled out for her.

"Charlie horse," she said to him.

"I understand. I have three daughters. I used to massage my wife's legs," he responded. He sat at his desk, and Rashad sat across from him.

Chelsea paced, reading the plaques on the wall and scanning the room while the men talked sale. She passed the desk, and an insurance policy caught her eye.

The insurance policy.

Chapter Twenty-two

Snap had fully intended to ask Belly-Belly out on a proper date. That woman was insanely fine. Pretty face and thick in all the right places. His kind of girl. But he realized after staring at her through a glass that she could also see through might have made him look like a lame groupie. So he decided to check up on Chelsea.

He started back down the hallway passing the door to Studio A just as Lee Bee was coming out. The two men gave each other a customary nod and walked down the hall in silence. Lee Bee was apparently headed to the supply closet while Snap continued to Mr. Harris' office.

The door was open. Snap looked inside and saw Chelsea standing beside Mr. Harris's desk with her head tilted. Snap knew what that meant. Rashad wasn't going to be purchasing the building.

"Shad," he said, getting his attention. Rashad looked up at the doorway. "Chelsea has something to say."

"Chelsea!" Rashad barked when he saw her face.

Chelsea snapped out of her trance, picked up a paper from his desk and looked at Mr. Harris. "You're selling this dump for $250,000, but you recently insured it for only $50,000."

There it is.

But before Mr. Harris could protest Chelsea's obvious implication, a loud scream came from the hallway. Startled, Snap looked and saw that Lee Bee was backing out of the supply closet. He was pointing and speechless.

Snap ran down the hallway to see what was in the closet. A man's body was slumped in the corner next to a mop bucket. He was bloody and obviously dead.

Chapter Twenty-three

Chelsea called Carter. He sent a patrol car to secure the scene. The cops quartered everyone off. Chelsea, Snap, Lee Bee and Mr. Harris were in the office. Half of Studios A and B ran out the building when they heard someone dropped a body in a closet. They weren't eager to speak with the police, based on previous dealings with law enforcement. Those who stayed, several of whom were too high to react fast enough, were quartered off into the studios. And then the cops started asking basic questions: Who are you? What are you doing here? When did you arrive?

After about two hours, the forensics team showed up. The medical examiner followed with Carter and Totty not far behind.

If you had asked her that morning, Chelsea would have said that it was impossible for Carter to embarrass her. He was her brother, and she loved him. One of her earliest memories was sharing a bath and splashing water on him. But when she saw him walking down the long hallway of the studio, all she could do was cringe. He'd always been a flamboyant dresser. Always doing too much. In 2005, he never left the house in any color other than DipSet pink. He had ruined a lot of shirts trying to dye them. Then he went through a bizarre Andre 3000 phase where he wore Ray's old dress pants and suspenders. He was a teenager and got a pass. But this suit was the end. It was so beige and so tight. Chelsea looked at Snap, whose mouth was agape in horror. What was Carter wearing and why?

Lee Bee only asked, "Is that your brother?" But what Chelsea heard was, "What's wrong with your family?"

Chelsea answered the question she heard.

"I don't know. I blame my stepmother."

Carter approached them with professionalism and valor. "Is everyone alright? I know you've all experienced a terrible shock. We just need you guys to answer a few questions for us. Can we do that?"

Normally, Chelsea would have taken pride in her brother's work ethic and take-charge attitude. She might have even snapped a picture to send to her father and Great Aunt Grace with a playful caption like, Look at Car doing his thing! But she couldn't get past his ensemble.

He hugged Chelsea. "I know seeing a dead body can shake you up. But it's okay. You're safe." He thought they were in shock because of the corpse? Nobody was upset about the dead body except Lee Bee, who kept insisting he only screamed because he was caught off-guard.

Before Chelsea could get the obvious question out of her mouth, Rashad roared, "What the hell you got on, Car? Who too-little suit is that? You look like the dude that hold the umbrella for P-Diddy."

Carter's partner, Totty, snickered and dropped her head so he couldn't see her. But he had heard her. And that was the end of his sympathy.

"Rashad, this better not be your fault," he yelled.

"Me?" Rashad asked, clearly offended. "Why would it be my fault? I don't kill people! I'm a businessman!"

"Mogul," Chelsea corrected sarcastically.

"That's right! Mogul. And moguls don't have time for this! My artists need to be recording them hit records," Rashad responded, missing the sarcasm.

Lee Bee looked strangely at Rashad. "Say what?"

Snap nudged Chelsea and pointed at Totty. They had heard about Carter's new partner and even read about her, but seeing her in person was something different. Her plain Ellen Degeneres suit and clean face didn't hide her real beauty or her curvaceous body. If she wasn't a cop, she could be a model for one of those booty magazines. She had the look of a woman that only dated professional athletes and partied five nights a week. It was cliché, but Chelsea wondered if she had ever been in any rap videos.

Snap, in true Black male form, unable to allow an attractive girl to work unbothered, said, "Forget about that dead guy, who is this beautiful woman and why is she with you?"

"Don't embarrass Car," Chelsea said.

But it was too late. Rashad was already breathing down on Totty. "Damn, girl. You fine. You don't need this little job. I can take care of you."

Carter sighed. Snap laughed out loud. Chelsea couldn't help but chuckle.

Totty impolitely pushed Rashad to the side. "Who found the body?"

Lee Bee raised his hand.

"Let's start with you. Carter, find out if there are any surveillance cameras. We need to see who fled the scene."

After Lee Bee explained how he stumbled on the body, Totty released him back into the hallway and took Mr. Harris off for a chat. Carter had discovered there were no working cameras on the dilapidated building but had begun interviewing the men and lady in the studio to find out who ran away. It would take days to track them all down.

Chelsea stood in the hallway with Snap and Lee Bee watching the forensic team lift fingerprints and collect all the blood samples. As was her inevitable way, she listened to every word she heard and gathered them in her brain. It was starting to get chaotic up there. She knew Mr. Harris was trying to scam Rashad; the insurance policy had proved that. But then somebody found a dead body, people started running, and the police showed up. And something about the whole thing seemed off.

"I hope this isn't too much stress on the baby," Lee Bee said kindly to Chelsea.

"We're fine," she responded. "It's just a murder."

Lee Bee laughed. "What brings you to this murder?"

"My stepbrother, Rashad, thought he was buying this building today. But that Harris guy is trash."

"Who is he? And why was he giving yaw a tour?"

Chelsea looked up at him in question. "He owns the building. How do you not know him?"

"This isn't our home studio. We followed our producer over here a couple of months ago. He charges us a flat rate, and we drop an envelope in his door slot once a month. We come in through the back door. And we're usually leaving out in the middle of the night. I ain't never seen the owner," he answered.

"So, Harris doesn't own your contract? Your music?" Chelsea asked.

"Own? Hell no. We're independent. We don't have no contracts with nobody." Lee Bee was looking at her as if she had just asked the world's stupidest question.

"Does this mean I can't meet Belly-Belly?" Snap jumped into their conversation.

Lee Bee laughed and shook his head. "Everywhere we go somebody wanna meet Bell. Dude, it's not hard. I'll introduce you as soon as your friends let her out of the lab." Rappers often referred to the studio as the lab. It made what they do sound scientific and even a little magical.

The revelation that there were no contracts just explained why the tour ended so abruptly after Lee Bee thanked Rashad for the champagne. It also cleared up a bit of the chaos and freed up some brain space to learn more about this sexy beast in front of her. His hair was, in her opinion, perfection. "What's it like managing a rapper?" she asked.

"It's cool. Most people don't know this, but Mag is huge in Europe. So part of the perks is I get to visit some cool places. We get treated in Barcelona the way 2-Chains gets treated here."

"Wow. That sounds amazing. You like Europe?"

"It's awesome. I mean, don't get me wrong, we some East Side brothers. My heart will always be at 7 Mile and Van Dyke. But I can't lie, being international is a wonderful feeling."

Chelsea smiled. She had low expectations of the type of people she'd meet when she'd left her house that morning. She'd prepared herself for criminals and hustlers. And here she met a man that'd been all over Europe.

She wanted to ask more questions about Lee Bee's travels but was interrupted by the forensics team placing the dead man's body on a gurney. She watched the medical examiner beckon for Carter.

Snap covered Chelsea's eyes. "You don't need to be looking at that."

She moved his hand.

"There's no ID on the vic, but we'll run his fingerprints," the ME said.

"What can you tell me about him?" Carter asked.

"Black male, looks to be in his mid-forties. He was stabbed in the back. The knife was still in him. He died quickly, didn't put up a fight."

"Anything interesting about the body?" Carter asked, taking notes.

"Not really. He has some calluses on his left hand, maybe he's a handyman or the janitor. I'll be able to tell you more after I get him on the table," the man said as he zipped the body bag over the dead guy's face.

"He doesn't work for me, Detective," Mr. Harris shouted down the hallway. He had also been standing in the hall waiting to be released. Carter looked up and acknowledged Mr. Harris.

Who was this unidentified man? And what was he doing in the 6 Million Ways studios that got him killed? Was he a rapping janitor? There were so many people in the building. Did he come with a friend? Where is the friend now? How could anybody know who had stabbed this man? It was all so confusing.

Totty had taken one of the smaller rooms for interviews. She and Rashad had been inside about ten minutes when the door opened, and she charged down the hallway toward Carter.

"Is this really your stepbrother?" she asked him.

"Technically," he answered, still jotting his notes.

"Captain might call this a conflict of interest. Your sister and friend are witnesses, and your stepbrother is holding a bag of money," she said with a slight attitude. "I have to call it in."

"You're the supervisor, Totty. You can make the decision," he said in protest.

"I can not, Detective French. We gotta do this one by the book. Not only is he related to you, but he is an heir to a huge fortune! That's going to bring the press down on our heads!"

"Fine!" Carter and his tiny suit stormed outside.

Chelsea felt bad for her big brother. It was her fault he was there. But it never occurred to her their presence would create a conflict for Carter. What difference did it make anyway? Carter was honest.

Lee Bee had taken a call and walked away leaving Chelsea dangling in the hallway. She wandered back into the office. She was finally ready to sit. She was feeling a little bit of heartburn and could taste the bacon from that morning. She bypassed the uncomfortable chair and went straight for Harris' comfy leather roller. She plopped down and spun around until she was facing the putting green and the golf clubs.

The golf clubs.

Chelsea went over and pulled a club out of the bag. She held it like she was a golfer and took a fake swing. She put it back in the bag and walked into the hallway. Lee Bee was still on the phone, and Snap was talking to a girl. Some of the chaos in her mind was clearing up. And the pieces were starting to fit together.

Chapter Twenty-four

Snap had finally gotten some face time with Belly-Belly, but he couldn't enjoy it. At first, everything was good. Well, at least as good as it could be after a murder. The investigation was moving along. Totty and the other officers had gotten a statement from everyone, not that anyone had much to say. When Belly-Belly had finished giving her statement, Lee Bee was cool enough to introduce her to Snap. She didn't mind that he was staring at her. She had been wondering who he was. It should have been the best moment of his life. A beautiful and famous woman was sending crazy signals his way. But he was distracted by Chelsea's tilted head.

The head tilts. He had seen her do it a million times. It meant her mind was working. It meant she was figuring something out. But it wasn't always a big deal. She used to do the tilt in Algebra class. She did it when she played cards. And the tilt always came out whenever he or Carter tried to surprise her. Then there were times when it was more intense. Like when Michael Simpson would lie on Carter. Or Mr. Harris leaving an insurance policy on the desk. The difference was the face scrunch.

The scrunch was a nose wrinkle, kind of like catching a bad odor. When the tilt met the scrunch, Chelsea was on to something big. The longer she stayed in the trance of tilting and scrunching, the more she had to think out. And the bigger the catch. Her current state of tilt was distracting Snap from his conversation with Belly-Belly.

"I'm hosting this party at Club Innocence tomorrow night. You should come."

"Oh, yeah. I'm there," Snap responded, looking over Belly-Belly's shoulder and directly at Chelsea.

Belly-Belly turned around. "Is she retarded?"

It wasn't uncommon for someone seeing Chelsea's quirk for the first time to be perplexed by the oddity and jump to that conclusion.

"No, she's a genius," he answered calmly.

"Fa real?"

"Yeah. Let's just say that if Sherlock Holmes lived in the ghetto and was a pregnant black woman, it would be Chelsea."

Belly-Belly's eyes got big. "She's that smart?"

"And that crazy."

"So what do that make you?"

He watched Chelsea's face relax to a smile. She knew who killed that man. He smiled back at her. "Sit tight, Baby, I gotta go be Watson for a minute. I'll be right back."

He needed to find Carter. He winked at Chelsea as he walked past her. "The case of the body in the closet."

Chapter Twenty-five

Carter had gotten the look straight from the pages of GQ Magazine. His personal shopper at Neiman Marcus had had to special order the tan Valentino suit with the cropped pants, and it wasn't cheap.

What did these fashion heathens know about clothes, anyway? He had always been one of the more stylish detectives on the squad, although some would say Sergeant Detective Howie Bell was the better dresser, just because his alligator shoes always matched his colorful suits with the extra-long jackets. But that wave of haberdashery had gone out with the last season of the Steve Harvey show. Not the talk show, but the sitcom he had with Cedric the Entertainer.

Carter stood outside and watched as rookie officers roped off the exterior of the building with crime scene tape. The forensic team was also about, collecting evidence. He remained unbothered by their snickers and wisecracks about his pants. There was a dead body inside the building. That was much more important. Besides, he was killing it, they didn't know.

Totty approached him. "Captain made the call. I tried to talk him out of it, but he wouldn't budge. He doesn't want the appearance of anything inappropriate. Adrian and Woo are taking over. And we get to watch from the sidelines."

Carter shrugged. "Thanks for trying. My family is going to be the death of my career."

"You sure it won't be those pants? They're awful tight," Totty teased, trying to break the tension.

"Ha, ha. It wouldn't hurt you to be a little more fashion-savvy," he offered.

"No, thank you. I get enough attention. I'll stick to my plain blue suits. Could you imagine if I tried to get sharp? Mitch Albom already calls me Chief Craig's 'side of bacon' whenever he sees me."

"They sure got here fast." Carter watched Woo park his SUV under a shady tree in front of the building. He and Adrian got out and walked up to the building. Adrian shook his head at Carter.

"What's up with the fit, Fam?" Woo asked, referring to Carter's unusual suit. "Not used to seeing this much ankle."

"Take those pants back to the store and get your ten dollars refunded," Adrian added.

"This suit was eighteen hundred. That's about your take-home pay after your child support garnishments, right, A?"

"They saw you coming. Anyway, why are you here?"

"It's their crime scene," Woo answered.

"Then why are we here?"

Totty wasn't in the mood for another one of Carter's and Adrian's arguments. "We arrived on the scene and learned a black male, forties, was found in a closet inside this music studio. No identification. Still waiting for the prints to come back. We began interviewing witnesses and realized we have a conflict. Captain reassigned the case to you and your partner. Is that good enough for you, Detective Gonzalez?"

"What conflict?" Woo asked.

Totty waited for Carter to comment, but she could see his reluctance. She gave him an encouraging nod.

"My stepbrother is inside. He was here on business." "Stepbrother?" Adrian asked. "As in, the son of your millionaire stepmother? I assume that's his Bentley over there?"

Carter nodded. "And Chelsea's with him."

Adrian rolled his eyes and twisted his mouth. "She'd better not get in my way."

"She won't try to do your job. She knows better," Carter said.

"Right. She doesn't know how to investigate a murder. At best, you have a very observant eyewitness. Make sure her statement is useful to you," Totty added. Even if she was taken off the case, she had seniority, and they had to listen to her.

"I agree. She might have noticed something," Woo interjected.

Carter saw Snap standing in between his squad car and the Bentley. He gave Carter a distinctive nod to get his attention.

"Chelsea's not a basset hound. She doesn't find clues. She won't be a good witness," Carter said.

"What do you mean?" Totty asked.

"She either knows who did it, or she doesn't. If she knows, it will be up to us, the professionals, to figure out how," Carter said, feeling at the snug pockets for his vibrating phone.

He pulled his phone out and saw a text message from Snap. The two words in the text changed his entire mood. He was still disappointed he couldn't work on the case, but at least now he knew Adrian would soon be very unhappy.

Snap had sent him a text message:

She knows.

Carter tried to hide his glee, but his muffled snicker quickly multiplied into a full-throated laugh.

"What's he laughing at?" Woo asked Totty.

"Probably his suit," Adrian answered.

"Hey, Car, where's the joke?" Totty was using her seniority voice again.

"No joke. I'm going to fall back and leave you gentlemen to your investigation. Totty, you should probably stay and help. I'm the conflict, not you." Carter had sobered his tone.

"And what will you be doing?" she asked.

"I'm going to go take a selfie in my Valentino suit, leaning against my stepbrother's car. Hashtag BoutThisLife. I'll be trending by the end of the day, promise." Carter walked away from the group like Tyson Beckford on a runway stage. Had he been wearing a hat, he most certainly would have tipped it.

"I hate that guy," Adrian said.

"I want a selfie with the car," Woo and Totty said in unison.

Chapter Twenty-six

Now that Chelsea had figured out what had happened to that poor murdered man, she needed some help. First of all, Carter needed to make sure Rashad didn't give away $250,000. He was so determined to buy a studio. In between interviews, he was still trying to close the deal. She had even heard him raise the price. He needed a parent.

Snap came back inside. "Adrian is taking over for Carter."

The two shared a look of disgust as the front door opened. Adrian, Woo, and Totty came down the hallway carrying all the authority of the Detroit Police Department.

"What are you going to do?" Snap asked Chelsea.

"Tell them, I guess."

Adrian approached Chelsea with his hand in his pocket and his suit jacket swinging behind him. "I don't care who your brother is. You step out of line at MY crime scene, and I will throw your hood rat ass in jail. We have your statement. Now stay out of the way."

Snap stepped up. "Yaw better get your boy!"

Adrian and Snap both postured in a fighting position.

"You can go to jail too!" Adrian said before Woo stood in between the men.

"Hey man, didn't we just say we were going to interview her? What's wrong with you?" Woo asked, irritated.

"We don't need this little ghetto girl! It's a room full of rappers. One of them is guilty!" Adrian said.

"Well maybe you can go talk to one Detective Gonzalez," Totty said, shaking her head in frustration.

Adrian sneered at Chelsea as he walked away. Woo turned back toward her. "Well, Shorty? Do you know anything?" he asked her straight.

"Not a thing," Chelsea said. "We were in the office when ol' boy found the body. We don't know these people. Right, Devin?"

Snap hesitated but then said, "Nah, we ain't see nothing."

Woo and Totty shrugged and walked away.

"I don't know if that was the right thing, Chels," Snap whispered.

"It's staring them in the face. They'll figure it out. They don't need a hoodrat."

"Where did Belly go?" Snap scanned the hallway until he found her down near the studios. And then he walked that way.

Adrian was right. She was just a girl from the block. And she could've been wrong about the whole thing. He would just make her feel worse if she was. It's not like she lied. She didn't know any of these people and had no reason to participate. She decided to mind her business and leave this murder to the police.

Chapter Twenty-seven

Totty should have been focusing on the investigation. But there was something about the French family that was distracting her thoughts and drowning out the sound of Adrian's voice. First, there was Carter's carefree exit from the conversation and his apparent joy with being kicked off the case. Then Totty observed the friend, Snap, casually talking to some rapper chick as if there was no dead body. She overheard the stepbrother just minutes before, still trying to complete the business transaction with the white guy. And now Chelsea was standing in the hallway having what appeared to be a flirtatious conversation with Lee Bee while fiddling with her iPhone. Something was up. And Totty intended to find out what.

She walked away from Adrian mid-sentence and approached Chelsea. Grabbing her by the arm, she pulled her away from Lee Bee. Chelsea tried to pull her arm back, but Totty was stronger than she looked.

"I heard about you, Chelsea!"

"You ain't heard nothin'," Chelsea said struggling. "Let me go. Where's Carter?"

Totty released her grip on Chelsea's forearm. "I'm sorry. But I feel like you know more than you're telling."

"You can feel however you want. But keep your hands off me."

"Chelsea, do you know something?" Totty asked sincerely. "Something that could help?"

"I know this is my last off day. And I've been stuck here for hours. I want to go home."

"Tell me something, and I'll let you go." Totty glanced over Chelsea's shoulder to see Lee Bee deeply engaged in their conversation. "You got something to say, sir?" she asked him in a threatening tone.

Lee Bee dropped his eyes and turned his head.

"Why are you here, Chelsea? You tryin' to rap now?"

"Rashad asked me to come. I already told you that."

"But why? Because you're a human lie detector? Because you're Sherlock Holmes?" Totty remembered that's how her peers had described Chelsea that night in the bar.

"Rashad is gullible. He was trying to buy the building, and I wanted to make sure he wasn't getting played."

"And was he?"

Chelsea shrugged. The Snap guy approached and put his arm around her. "What's going on, Chels?" he asked.

"The Hottie thinks I'm hiding something." She looked Totty squarely in the face. Snap said nothing in return. He turned away for a second then turned back, never quite making eye contact with her.

Snap's reaction spoke volumes to an experienced investigator like Totty. "I may not be a human lie detector. But I do know two shifty suspects when I see them."

"Suspects?" Snap asked in shock. "How are we suspects?"

"Why else hide what you know? You must be protecting someone. And the only person it could be is Rashad. Well, I'll take him down to the station and get it out of him."

"Wait! No," Snap said before turning Chelsea toward him. "You can't let Shad go to jail."

"So you do know? Why would you let us waste time? And don't say shit to me about snitching! You are the sister of a police officer."

"I'm also a hoodrat," Chelsea said defiantly.

Totty exhaled deeply before speaking. "That was Adrian's opinion, not mine. We both know what a d-bag he is. I would appreciate anything you have to offer this investigation."

166

So little Chelsea was teaching the Detroit Police Department a lesson. But would she let a killer go free just to prove her point?

"Chelsea, I'm sorry that Adrian was rude to you. And I know you two have a history. I don't doubt he loved saying that, just like you love this little payback now. But there is a dead man that deserves justice. Don't you want us to catch the killer?" Totty implored.

"He ain't going nowhere. Carter's watching Rashad."

"So it is Rashad?" Totty turned to beckon for Woo and Adrian.

"No. It isn't. But he has $250,000 in a bag. Killer won't leave without it. That's what this is all about."

Woo approached the group, but Adrian saw that it was Chelsea he was being called to and was determined to ignore her. Instead, he lagged behind and started talking to a forensic tech.

"What you got?" Woo asked.

"She knows who did it," Totty said.

"Like seriously? Well, who is it?"

Snap nudged his friend, who was still reluctant to speak. She looked up at him; he nodded at her. She turned toward the detectives.

"It's our fault for always assuming the white man must own the building. The rappers never saw the owner. He came in the mornings, they worked mostly at night. He kept his door closed when he was in his office. They paid him through a slot in the door. So all a scammer would have to do is walk into the building, sit at that desk, and say he was the owner."

"Are you saying Steven Harris doesn't own the building?" Totty asked.

"I'm saying, Steven Harris is the dead guy. I don't know who that white man is. But if I had to guess, I'd say he's an insurance salesman. Rashad was about to hand him a quarter of a million dollars in cash, and that was worth killing for."

Totty's face froze in surprise. She was speechless. That never happened.

"What? How?" Woo asked.

Chelsea sighed like she was annoyed that no one else understood. "Those are left-handed golf clubs in the office. The medical examiner said the victim had calluses on his left hand. There's a plaque on the wall for a father and son tournament. But that white dude told us that he had three daughters. Don't you get it? He's not Harris. The dead guy must be."

"So he got here before we did, and killed the real Steven Harris, who probably wasn't even trying to sell the building," Snap said.

"That would explain three things: One, why the tour was so quick. Two, how Shad thought he was buying contracts that were never for sale. And three, for a guy trying to make a quick sale why nothing was packed up," Chelsea added.

Totty looked at Woo, and knew what he was thinking. Eyes wide, with a serious tone he said to Chelsea, "Does Carter know?"

Because if he did, Totty was going to kill him. It's one thing for his bratty kid sister to muck up the works, but for her very own partner to watch them chase their tails for the last three hours was unforgivable.

"No. You're the first person I said anything to. I can prove it." Chelsea first swiped up, then over, then down before handing Totty her phone.

"Keep your eye on the white guy. And don't let Rashad give him the bag," Totty read aloud, "I don't trust him."

Carter had responded: Okay.

"So he just thought you were talking about the purchase, or at least that's what he'll tell the Captain," Woo said.

Chelsea's half-smile affirmed his theory.

"You would have eventually figured it out," she said, unremorseful.

"I ought to arrest you," Totty snapped back. She was livid that Chelsea would sit on these vital clues, and still offended at the flippancy with which she had called her "the hottie".

"You're the murder police, not us. You get a paycheck for this. She didn't have to help you at all," Snap responded with a curt edge to his tone. It was evident that the French clan felt some entitlement because of Carter.

"Find Carter and Mr. Harris or whatever his name is," Woo directed to one of the patrol officers in the hallway.

"You owe me two hours of my life back."

"Well, when you take all the credit, we'll be even," Chelsea said sarcastically.

In the exact moment that Totty could see herself slapping Chelsea across the face for being so disrespectful, Adrian finally approached the group.

"Stop wasting time over here with them," he said, referring to Chelsea and Snap. "There's a rapper here named Killer Kon who, if you ask me, might be the number one suspect. Something about him is rubbing me the wrong way. I think we should take him down to the station and put him in the hot box until he tells us what happened here."

Woo looked at Adrian and shook his head. It was obvious he was embarrassed by his partner. But no one said a word. Adrian looked at his fellow officers and then noticed Chelsea's smug expression.

"Again?!" he asked, annoyed.

Woo and Totty walked off, leaving Adrian and Chelsea to exchange snarly looks. They found Rashad and the fake Harris chatting near the back door with Carter keeping a watchful eye.

Woo approached the men with a big smile. "Mr. Harris, we need to ask you some additional questions downtown."

The fake Harris frowned.

Rashad was confused. "I just need five more minutes to close this deal, and then he's all yours."

Chapter Twenty-eight

"So? You get a date with her?" Chelsea asked Snap when he approached her in the parking lot about an hour after the insurance agent had been handcuffed and placed in the back of a squad car.

Chelsea had been right. Steven Harris had given his insurance agent a tour of his studio early one morning before purchasing a policy. When that guy met Rashad at The Henry a couple of weeks later, he hatched a plan to separate a pigeon from $250,000. The only thing standing in the way of his grift was the real Mr. Harris. The grifter expected to be gone and off the grid before anyone found the body. It was just his misfortune that Lee Bee opened the closet when he did.

"Nah. I can't date her. She ain't my type. She actually asked was you mentally disabled. I don't think she could hang with us. She still fine though," Snap answered. "Where is Rashad? I'm hungry."

Lee Bee approached the friends. "You knew he was the killer the whole time?"

"No," Chelsea answered. "Something was off when I got in the office. But I just thought he was trying to trick Rashad. It wasn't until after the medical examiner showed Car the calluses that I figured out the rest."

"Why didn't you say anything?" he asked her, perplexed.

"I would've told my brother, but they took him off the case before I had a chance. And I wouldn't help that Adrian solve a crossword puzzle," she said plainly.

"So if the thick one hadn't cornered you, then what?" The 'thick one' referring to Totty. As if she needed another nickname.

"I don't know." She turned to Snap. "That was trippy. One minute I'm kicking it with Lee and the next she's all in my face. Where did that come from?"

"Maybe your exploits have made their way around the station," Snap offered.

"This isn't the first time you've done this?" Lee Bee asked.

Chelsea shrugged.

"That was the dopest thing I've ever seen. I am impressed. We should exchange numbers." He had stepped closer to her and stared into her eyes, kind of flirty.

She smiled up at him. He was a cutie. "You'll tell me about Barcelona?"

"I'll tell you about all the places I've been. When you're ready, I may even take you with me."

Chelsea rubbed her stomach, "Not sure if I'll be able to travel anytime soon."

Lee Bee began to rub Chelsea's stomach too. Usually, she didn't like when people did that, but this time she just giggled. The two became so entrenched in their plans of world travel that neither noticed when Snap walked away.

Until Rashad walked up. "Man, this is messed up. I was supposed to be a mogul today."

"What did Birdman say?" Chelsea said, winking at Lee Bee.

"He told me to find another building and get my weight up." Rashad was giving mad gloomy face.

"That's good advice," Lee Bee said.

"But I wanted to be a mogul today!" Rashad whined.

Chelsea smacked her lips. "Shad, it's time to get that car off this block. Let's go." She waved goodbye to Lee Bee and pulled a listless Rashad to his vehicle.

Chapter Twenty-nine

Amir Ali sat at his desk in a back room of Farmer Roger's, shaking his head while listening to the corporate IT guy explain that the system will be down for at least two hours.

"This is very, very bad," he said in a thick Arabic accent. "I will soon have store fill with customer." He continued to shake his head at whatever was on the other end. "Very, very bad." He hung up the phone and looked at most of his opening staff. The ones that had arrived to work on time and were awaiting word on the malfunctioning cash registers.

"Registers will be offline for at least two hour."

The staff began to groan but none more loudly than Mr. Ali's son, Adi, the 21-year-old upstart being forced to work at his father's store in exchange for his extravagant lifestyle. "I guess I have to stay up front today to keep you guys from stealing."

Shaun Orr took offense at Adi's crack and asked, "Yo, what's that supposed to mean?"

Adi Ali shifted uncomfortably. He didn't want to spar with the muscle-bound meat manager today. "I'm just saying. We will lose a lot of money today, Baba."

Mr. Ali was often embarrassed by his obnoxious son. Most of his employees had been with him since he purchased the franchise grocery store. He was fortunate in having low turnover. He treated his employees as fairly as he could afford. He offered better wages than other stores in the neighborhood and even provided healthcare benefits for his senior employees. He didn't worry about his morning staff stealing while the system was down. He was afraid of losing customers.

"Always making some crack about Black people," Deuxie Fontaine said. She was the oldest member of the staff. "Like he ain't trying to pick up every Black girl with a big booty and a EBT card that walk in this sto'."

That was also true.

"Where is Chelsea?" Mr. Ali asked, realizing his favorite employee was not there to offer a solution and silence his son.

Adi, without the accent but with every ounce of entitlement afforded to wealthy kids raised in America said, "She's late again. She's always late."

"You walk to work six months pregnant and see what time you get here," Dolores said. She was the bakery manager.

She used to be Miss Madeleine's best friend before the number hit. To hear her tell it, it was her dream that gave Maddy the winning numbers that would forever change her life and make her a woman of wealth and leisure. They had since stopped being friends.

"If I have to get up and be to work on time, then so does she. It is not fair to the rest of us, right?" Adi pleaded with his co-workers to have someone on his side, just once.

Chelsea stood in the doorway of Mr. Ali's office, tying her apron around her back. "It's not fair that your friends get to park in the back, enter through the loading dock, and leave with beer."

Mr. Ali clapped his hands together. "Thank goodness you are here. I feared Babe had you laid up with swollen ankles again. This is a very, very bad day."

As he filled her in on the mainframe malfunctions, Chelsea nodded along to all of his technical talk and retail jargon. Mr. Ali had come to this country to be an engineer. Sometimes when he was speaking to his staff, he would drift into overly technical computer language. Usually, Chelsea would just look over at the junior Ali.

"You can scan the UPCs for inventory, but you have to enter the price manually."

"Well, you might as well close the store, because I ain't doing all that," one of the cashiers, Shameka, said, lips smacking while drinking a Faygo Redpop for breakfast.

"What about credit cards and checks?" Adi asked, ignoring Shameka. He was the customer service manager and would be the one fielding most of the complaints for the next two hours.

"Working fine," Mr. Ali reassured his staff.

"Who can remember what everything cost in this store?" Shameka fussed.

Everyone looked at Chelsea.

"No problem," she responded. "I just need the new sales paper." And that's why Chelsea was Mr. Ali's favorite employee, and her chronic lateness was never a problem. Her photographic memory was about to save him thousands of dollars. Sure, a few customers would challenge her, but she would be right.

"Baba, you can't!" Adi said.

"Adi, shut your face up and get Chelsea a sales paper," the senior Ali barked.

Having the largest Arab population outside of the Middle East had affected race relations in Detroit. Most small grocery stores and gas stations were owned and operated by Arab-Americans. And a significant number of those stores were in

African-American neighborhoods like Chelsea's. The two communities had lived together for decades and had to come to an unspoken understanding. The definition of Islamophobia was limited to fear of gas prices increasing. And the neighborhood dope dealers were scarier than the Alt-Right. As much as Adi regularly irked everyone, if disgruntled customers attacked his ethnicity or questioned his patriotism, his co-workers would always say, "Adi's not a terrorist. He's just an asshole. He don't want to hurt nobody." Like most blacks in Detroit, they knew the difference. A fact men and women like Mr. Ali were grateful for nowadays.

Adi handed Chelsea the current sales paper. She blew him a kiss. "Thank you, Adi. I'ma name my baby after you."

Chapter Thirty

After spending two hours as the only cashier for Farmer Roger's franchise store number 41, the system was restored and Shameka took over the register to give Chelsea a break. Usually, she would take 15 to 30 minutes to rest her feet and read baby names in the employee lounge, but today she wanted some sun and donuts. Donut Town was across the street from Farmer Roger's. It was just a two-minute walk if she caught the light. She couldn't wait to get her hands on two buttermilk donuts, one chocolate cake, and a jelly-filled cream. She left out the front entrance of the store, turned right toward Joy Road, and walked past Martha's Soul Food Restaurant which was adjacent to Farmer Roger's, located in the same shopping complex separated by only one wall. She was on a donut mission and not paying attention to any of the other people walking in the parking lot. The last person she expected to see was Carter's partner, Totty Bester, leaving the restaurant.

"Chelsea!" she called out.

A startled Chelsea looked up and waved. She hoped she could pass Totty quickly and without conversation.

"Wait." Totty approached with a smile that Chelsea didn't understand. Their last encounter had not been pleasant.

"What a surprise!"

"I work here," Chelsea said with all the warmth of a Michigan winter.

"God, why? If I had a stepmother..."

Chelsea cut her off. "You need something? I only get a few minutes for my break."

"I'm glad I ran into you. I thought we should talk about what happened at the crime scene." She paused as she tried to find her words. "I've been on the force for thirteen years. I've seen a lot of death, and I've helped bring a lot of killers to justice. But I've never met anyone like you."

"What is that supposed to mean?" Chelsea said with an attitude.

"You're so gifted and so angry. I don't doubt you have reason to be. And your life is about to have a new set of challenges." Totty pointed to Chelsea's stomach. "But I think we, as Black women, have to do better. We have to help and support each other. I believe in your gift. And I just want you to know that if you need anything, I'm here for you."

Chelsea wasn't expecting Totty's words to move her. She could feel the tightness in her jaws relaxing. "Look, girl. I'm alright. And I'm gon' be alright. I appreciate you though."

Totty nodded. "Okay, well, just so you know, if you need me, I'm here." She handed Chelsea a business card. "Put my number in your phone."

Chelsea took the card and began to feel guilty about their last meeting. "I'm sorry I didn't say anything about the murder. I let Adrian get inside my head."

"It's okay. We put a killer away, and we couldn't have done it without your help. And I'll never be too proud to ask you for it."

Chelsea finally smiled at Totty.

"Can I have a hug? The way your brother talks about you, I was hoping we could be friends," Totty asked shyly. Chelsea stepped closer to her with her arms outstretched, and the two women embraced.

"Hey, Chelsea."

Again she was startled to hear someone say her name. When she turned around, she saw Romeo Qadir coming toward her, carrying a take-out container from Martha's. She was surprised to see him.

"Romeo? What are you doing so far away from English Village?" Chelsea said, referring to the east side neighborhood that Romeo called home.

"Totty and I had lunch." he reached in for an awkward hug. Chelsea didn't know that Romeo even knew Totty. Carter must have hooked them up. Why was the French family so determined to find Mr. Qadir a woman?

"May I?" he asked, motioning to rub her stomach. He hadn't seen her in about two years when she ran into him at Carter's condo. She had a waist then.

Chelsea put his hand on her stomach, and he began to make small circular motions. "It's nice to see you, Chels. You know my mother will want to see this baby," he said, reminding Chelsea of how kind and gracious his mother had been after her own mother had died. She had come to check on Chelsea every day for three weeks.

"I guess I hadn't realized that you two were friends," Totty said with just a pinch of venom in her voice. Romeo stopped rubbing.

"Ditto," Chelsea responded to Totty, not taking her eyes off Romeo. "Give Ms. Rashidah my best." But then she remembered her man was in jail, and her break was almost over. "I gotta go. It was nice seeing you both."

She charged towards Donut Town. Totty and Romeo walked toward the parked cars. Chelsea wondered if they'd ridden together like a real date or just met up at the restaurant. She turned back to look and saw Romeo chivalrously opening his passenger door for Totty.

Making the light, Chelsea was about 30 seconds from her donuts. She recalled her extraordinary evening with Romeo and pondered whether he was the one that got away. Or the one that would've made her miserable trying to change her.

Make that three buttermilk donuts, two chocolate cakes, and two jelly-filled creams.

Chapter Thirty-one

Lee Bee had called Chelsea that morning to invite her to his home for a late brunch with a few friends. He seemed genuinely fascinated with her after the incident at 6MW. He'd left the country for three weeks with his rap artist, MagNif, but had recently arrived back and wanted to see her.

Due to the expansion of her waistline and the spreading of her hips, she had nothing decent to wear. There was just enough time to get to Fairlane Mall for some shopping. She pulled the covers back and looked at her feet. They weren't swollen. Good. She could wear heels, not too high.

Once she was in the back of the Uber, she used Google to look through photo galleries of current fashion trends using the keywords apple shape, top heavy, and big stomach. She knew she wanted to wear leggings or something with an elastic waist. Buttons and zippers were torture for pregnant women, even the maternity clothes, which were all ugly.

Knowing exactly what she wanted to buy, she thanked her Uber driver and headed straight for the Mac Cosmetics store for lip gloss, then to the Pretti Pieces Boutique for a blouse she saw online and hoped they still had in stock. It was off the shoulders and empire-waisted. She couldn't hide her baby bump, but she could minimize it. Accessories, a new handbag, a Frappuccino, and finally a pair of not-too-high heels from DSW, and Chelsea was on her way home. It was so rare that she went out of her way for anything that she never felt guilty when she overspent. She liked Lee Bee and had a feeling his brunch would be worth the effort. Or maybe just not worth the embarrassment of no effort. He was a fly guy and his friends probably were too. Chelsea didn't want to be the tacky one at the table.

"You don't have to look like what you're going through," her mother, Diane, would always say when they were out shopping and she was buying something expensive that Ray French couldn't afford.

Chelsea sat at her vanity watching a YouTube hairstyling video. Her hair had gotten so long during pregnancy, and she didn't know what to do with it. She found a simple but elegant pinup style and was mimicking with care how to lay each strand. She was pinning the back when she noticed Carter standing in her doorway like he used to do when they were teens.

"I haven't seen you prettying up in a while. What are you doing today?"

"Remember that guy, Lee Bee, from the murder? He invited me to brunch."

"And you're going?" Carter asked, surprised.

"Yeah. He's nice."
"You meet a guy over a dead body and go on a date with him?"

"It's not a date. It's more like a day party. No big deal," Chelsea said, spritzing her bangs. "And I have to leave soon, so get out my room and let me dress."

She rose from her vanity and shut the door in his face. Just like when they were teens.

Chelsea could tell that Carter was a little envious when a Lexus SUV had arrived to pick her up.

"What's all this?" he asked, looking out the front window.

"Lee Bee insisted on sending me a car even though I told him I could just Uber."

"You have a car in the garage. Why do you always insist on pulling up everywhere in the backseat of somebody else's Malibu?"

"Oh, I'm not doing this with you today, Detective French." Chelsea added a hint of snootiness to her voice. "If you need me, I'll be brunching with friends in Midtown."

Three minutes later she was in the back of the Lexus, and her phone was chiming. She guessed it was Snap and was right. "Who Lexus was that in front of the crib? You kicking it with a Piston?" Snap teased, knowing Chelsea hated those supercilious pro-ball player types. The better they were on the court, the worse they were in real life.

"No, I'm going to eat with that guy Lee Bee, the manager from the studio."

"You didn't invite your boy? You just leaving me?"

"You didn't invite me last week when you went to Jobbie Nooner on Larry's boat." Jobbie Nooner was an annual boating event that began on the Detroit River and ended in Lake Erie. People all over town would call off work to sit in the sun and get drunk on the decks. This year Snap had opted to do that with their mutual friend Larry who had a boat...and many lady friends.

"Touché. But still..."

"Goodbye, Devin. I shall see you when I return." She was using her snooty voice again. She hung up and laughed to herself.

The Lexus pulled up to the Midtown Cooperative Lofts on Canfield Street. The doorman rushed out to open Chelsea's door and escort her into one of the many new and exclusive apartment buildings to come to Detroit. Gentrification was sweeping through downtown like the locusts in Egypt.

Chelsea remembered when this building was an abandoned warehouse. Now a doorman was pointing her toward a private elevator.

It was one of those remodels that still looked like a warehouse. That meant aesthetically unattractive on the outside but expensive. Each unit had an old industrial roll-up door. The kind you had to bend all the way down and push up to open. Lee Bee had installed a remote device to do that for him. She rang the doorbell, heard a series of beeps and waited for the door to roll up, first seeing just feet and then legs, and eventually his welcoming face. He leaned over to hug and kiss her cheek.

"Welcome, Chelsea. I'm so glad you could make it."

"Thank you for inviting me."

"Please come in and make yourself at home." He was pulling her by the hand. He whisked her into what was fashioned as a living room. It was hard to tell in loft spaces where one room ended and the next began. "Everybody, this is Chelsea."

There were four other people within earshot of his announcement. The only one to respond with any enthusiasm was the caterer in the kitchen area, who waved a spatula and said, "Hey, Miss Lady. Hope you brought your appetite."

"That's my Aunt Simply. She cooks for all my parties. She's the best there is."

"Hi, Aunt Simply," Chelsea said.

The other three seemed much less interested in Chelsea's arrival. Her hand still in his, he gently pulled her closer to the group.

"Chelsea, meet my friends." He started his introductions to her left. "This is Trillness, maybe you've heard of him. He's a vlogger. All things hip hop. His word on any EP is law."

Trillness extended a stoic hand to Chelsea.

"This is my homegirl, Mina. One day she'll be my lawyer." He was smiling. Mina was not. She appeared to be biracial, black and Asian. She wore her hair long and straight, bringing out her Asian bone structure and high cheekbones. She was dressed impeccably and stood with the confidence of a future attorney. And the conceit of a woman that knew she was beautiful.

"And last but not least, my oldest friend, Dionysius, but we just call him Si. I've known him since high school. He's like my brother."

"God of wine and song. Your mother wanted you to turn up," Chelsea said.

Si laughed. "Most people don't know that."

"I told you she was smart," Lee Bee said proudly.

"There was a girl in my fifth grade class named Artemis. You related?" Chelsea teased.

"How does a girl from MacKenzie High School know Greek mythology?"

"Must've read it somewhere. How did you know I went to MacKenzie?"

"Lee said he was sending the car to Plymouth and Wyoming. That's Stag country," Si said, referring to Mackenzie High's mascot.

"And Stags can't learn Greek mythology?"

"Not as well as we Technicians," he said arrogantly.

Cass Technical High School was one of Detroit's oldest and most prominent schools with a history of successful and annoying alumni.

"We all had the same textbooks, Bro," Chelsea laughed. Si joined in.

"You're right. Mina also went to Cass," he said.

"Who cares about high school? I'm about to get a law degree," she said flipping her hair and dripping her egotism.

Chelsea had a feeling she wasn't going to like Mina.

"What do you do?" Mina said to Chelsea. Her tone was very Lady of the Manor talking at Chelsea like she was the downstairs maid.

Chelsea placed her hand against her lower abdomen. "Where is the bathroom?" She didn't have to pee, but she found that the bigger her stomach got, the better of an excuse it became to get away from undesirable conversations.

Si pointed her in the direction. The bathroom could only be accessed by cutting through Lee Bee's bedroom. She noticed he shared her love of lavish pillows and Egyptian thread counts. Although, there was too much gray.

When she came back into the living room, Aunt Simply had gathered everyone around the table.

"Come on here, Little Momma. This food will not last." Her voice was warm and inviting.

Chelsea took a seat at the table in between Lee Bee and Trillness. Both men were already face down in a plate. Lee at least took his free hand to pull out the chair for her.

Aunt Simply had made quite a spread for these upwardly mobile twenty-somethings. There were chicken and waffles, homemade and not Eggo. Thick strips of bacon and eggs scrambled with mushrooms and avocado. And there was Mimosa that Chelsea wanted desperately. Instead, Lee Bee placed a champagne flute filled with freshly squeezed orange juice in front of her.

"You probably need this vitamin C," he said with his mouth full of waffles.

She nodded and took a sip. Aunt Simply placed a plate with mostly fruit and eggs in front of her. There was a chicken wing. And no waffle, not even a triangle.

"You don't need too much sugar in your condition. And no pork," Simply said maternally.

People had been telling Chelsea what to eat for the past few months. It was infuriating. But this was the first time someone had made her plate.

"I want a waffle," Chelsea said.

Everyone looked up from their plates and Aunt Simply turned midstep.

"You don't want to get fat. My oldest Vincent put twenty-five pounds on me."

"I want a waffle," Chelsea repeated.

Lee Bee offered her one of his. She took it.

"I can't blame you. Aunty can cook!" Trillness said.

Chelsea couldn't disagree. The first bite of that warm, buttery waffle made her smile. Food was one of the few pleasures she still had.

"Now you see why she does all my cooking for me," Lee Bee said, still chewing.

"I wish she would cook all my meals," Si said.

"I would be as fat as her." Mina was pointing to Chelsea with her fork and laughing. Chelsea offered a fake smile and reminded herself to be nice in her new clothes. Cass Tech didn't want none of this MacKenzie.

"At least I go to your house and help out, Aunty. I don't just eat your food up like your greedy nephew," Trillness said with a sly wink.

Lee Bee managed a smirk in mid-chew. "I go over and check up when I can. I can't help it if I'm out of town so much."

Chelsea sat in between the two men giggling at their sophomoric banter. She could feel the closeness between them. Carter and Snap often behaved the same way.

"Now don't get me wrong, I have always loved my nephew and his friends. But they come to my house and eat more than they help. And this one," she said, nudging Trillness, "just eats and leaves," Aunt Simply said, throwing her shade. The table erupted in laughter.

"Just make sure you take these leftovers with you. I'm about to start eating right. I can't have this fattening food around, or I'll eat it all tonight," Lee Bee added.

"Whatever, nephew, every week you tell me you're eating better," she teased.

"More for me," the portly Trillness said. "I'll be by later for another plate." He apparently wasn't trying to eat better.

Mina wiped her mouth like a finished lady, then laid the napkin in her lap. "So Lee, I love good food and everything. But, why did you ask us here today?"

"Yeah, Bro, what's really good? You only call us over when you have a major announcement," Si seconded.

"Well, you're all my team. Mina, when you get your law degree, you'll be able to do a lot more, but right now I appreciate the help you've done with contracts and copyrights. Trill, I know for a fact Magnif wouldn't be getting love in the streets if it wasn't for your social media. And Si, you already know, you're my right hand, my security, my promoter, my agent, whatever I need," he said emphatically.

"And what about her?" Mina flippantly threw her hand to her Chelsea, "She new to the team?

Chelsea was running out of patience with this stank bougie broad. She didn't have a good history with this type of woman.

The ones that were born and raised in Detroit not too far from her bad neighborhood, but felt superior to her because they attended Cass Tech and their fathers and mothers had better-paying jobs. As if everyone hadn't descended from housekeepers and train porters. But for some reason, she needed to look down on Chelsea. And Chelsea was trying to be cool because Lee Bee was cool. She wondered, did he have any idea how close she was to punching Mina in the face?

"Chelsea," Lee began, "is my new friend. I invited her to hang out with me and my old friends. Is that a problem?"

"Yeah. You don't have to always be mean, just 'cause yo name is Mina," Trillness said and laughed.

"I'm just saying..." Her voice trailed off.

"Answer the question, Lee!" Si said, cutting Mina off.

"I have something to show you," Lee said, finishing the last bit of bacon and waffle on his plate.

A few minutes later, Aunt Simply started scraping plates in the kitchen while the others took their mimosas in the living room.

"Aunty, I want you in here too. Clean up later," Lee said to her.

She put a plate back on the table and followed everyone to the living room.

Lee darted into his bedroom and came back out with a velvet pouch that was about the size of his hand. "Well, team and Chelsea, as you may know, Mag's album is doing very well in Europe. Sweden's number-one hip-hop magazine honored us last week with this." He pulled something bright and shiny from the velvet bag and held it up for his friends to see. It was an award in the shape of a microphone. The base was gold, the bulb encrusted with diamonds.

Everyone's pleased reaction of oohs and aahs brought a big smile to Lee Bee's face. Aunt Simply embraced him.

"I'm so proud of you, baby."

Trillness immediately began snapping pictures on his phone of the diamond mic while Mina squealed with delight. Chelsea felt honored that he included her in this intimate unveiling. Obviously, as Mina pointed out, she was not part of the team. It was flattering that he had invited her anyway.

"Mag wanted me to have it, because of all the hard work I do. But I feel like it belongs to all of us because I don't do it alone. It hasn't been easy grooming Mag for superstar status, and I know I couldn't have done it without you. So I wanted yaw to be the first to see it."

Mina managed to calm herself long enough to ask an important question. "Please tell me that it's insured? You can't just assume it's covered under your homeowners'. You have to get this appraised."

"Look at my professional girl thinking ahead," Lee Bee said, proud and smiling. "I promise to be very careful with it until I get it appraised."

"How much do you think it's worth?" Si asked.

"If I had to guess from all these diamonds, I'd say about twenty bands."

Chelsea couldn't pretend this was the first time she had seen diamonds that cost $20,000. Bejeweled necklaces and bracelets were the first thing Rashad had bought with his mother's newfound fortune. But since Lee and Magnif had earned this valuable possession, it was that much nicer than Rashad's bling.

"I think this calls for some real champagne!" Mina said as she downed the last of her mimosa.

Simply scurried back into the kitchen and pulled a fresh bottle of Ace of Spades out of Lee Bee's sub-zero refrigerator. Lee missed the sound of the cork popping because he had placed the diamond mic back in the velvet satchel and returned to his room to put it away. He reappeared just in time to accept a glass of the bubbly and raise a toast with his friends. Simply refilled Chelsea's orange juice. Chelsea would have preferred a

Pepsi, but she knew there would be a lecture about sugar and caffeine if she asked.

"Here's to Mag, me, and everybody in this room working hard for this dream. We started from the bottom. Seven Mile and Van Dyke, and look at us now!"

As the glasses came together in clink, Mina made a point of saying, "You may be from Seven Mile and Van Dyke, but I'm not." And then she laughed snobbishly.

Aunt Simply returned to the kitchen for cleanup while the champagne and conversation continued to flow in the living room. Si went out of his way to share a few embarrassing childhood stories about Lee. Mina was distracted by text messages and kept dropping her head to reply. She giggled. Must've been a man. Trillness went into the kitchen to help Aunt Simply clean, but ended up making himself another plate.

Three bottles of champagne later, Aunt Simply left the younger ones to their fun, taking her cooking gear and the leftovers with her. She was kind enough to leave Chelsea a giant carafe of freshly squeezed orange juice so that she could refill her glass at the same rate of speed as the alcohol drinkers. This, of course, caused Chelsea to have to make several runs to the bathroom.

On one such potty pursuit, Chelsea noticed as she left the bathroom that two of Lee Bee's dresser drawers were slightly open. She also saw the clock on his dresser said 4:40.

At 5 o'clock, Lee Bee - in the midst of Mina's bragging and shameless name-dropping - left the room seconds before a fascinating discovery.

"We always sit in the same box at the Palace," said Mina. "My cousin used to date Rip Hamilton, and he gets her tickets every year. But last week, Rashad Baker was sitting in the box next to us. And he has been blowing up my phone ever since. He can't stop texting me. He has millions that he can't wait to spend on me," she said, not knowing Chelsea was his stepsister.

Chelsea didn't believe her cousin had Rip Hamilton's tickets and wanted to call her out. It wasn't a head tilt kind of lie. More of her intuition. But then she mentioned Rashad, and instead, Chelsea just chuckled.

"What's so funny?" Mina asked, throwing major attitude.

"You. All this pomp and circumstances you've been giving us all day. Law school, I didn't grow up on Seven Mile, hoity-toity bougie blah, and you chasing Shad? It's hilarious."

Mina stood up and pointed her finger at Chelsea like she was going to fuss, but was interrupted by Lee Bee's panicked yelp. He came out of his bedroom holding the empty velvet satchel. "It's gone!"

"Well, what do you expect when you bring strangers around?" Mina said venomously.

"Start at the beginning. What happened?" Chelsea said calmly, ignoring Mina's crack. Her thing with Rashad had cost Mina all her elitist credibility.

"I went into the bedroom and noticed the drawer was slightly open. I checked, and the mic wasn't there." Lee's panic had turned to anger. His eyebrows furrowed, and his breaths became deep and rapid. He was staring intensely at his guests. One of them was a thief.

Chelsea was using the bathroom roughly every forty-five minutes. The drawer was open at 4:40, but not 4 PM. Chelsea guessed an approximate time of the theft.

Unfortunately, she wasn't watching the guests' every move. She had no idea who was in and out of the bathroom. The crime seemed impetuous and impulsive. Everyone, except Chelsea, was drunk. And she had been preoccupied with her full bladder. There was no shortage of opportunity.

"I think your little ghetto friend should empty her purse. And lift her breasts up. She could be hiding it in that curtain she's wearing. She probably needs that kind of money," Mina said viciously.

201

"Ain't you the one in law school? You need that kind of money, too." Chelsea was getting angry.

"She did keep going into your bedroom, Bro," Trillness offered softly.
"Because I'm pregnant! Not because I'm a thief!"
Chelsea picked up her champagne flute and threw it at Mina, who ducked in a nick, causing the flute to shatter on the floor. Si jumped up and stood between the women. Chelsea waddled around him and into the kitchen to get a broom. Lee Bee followed her.

"That was dramatic," he said, handing her the dustpan.

"I'm sorry," she offered remorsefully. "I'm sick of her."

"Forgive Mina. She's used to being the center of attention around here. The fellas treat her like royalty."

"Well, she's about to catch this coup if she keep talking to me crazy," Chelsea said frankly. "Look, you can check me. Not my boobs but my purse. I don't want you thinking for one minute that I would come to your home and steal from you. But then I'm leaving."

"No. You can't. I know you didn't steal anything. The truth is, one of my friends has been stealing from me for a while. I've been noticing things are missing. Cufflinks, a watch, a pinky ring, my iPad and even some cash. I've narrowed it down to those three people. So I showed them the diamond mic and hoped I could catch whoever it is."

"What? You set a trap?" Chelsea asked in a hushed tone.

"Yes. I need to know. And I need you to help me." He was emphatic.

"Is that why you invited me over here?"

"I've seen your work. If you could solve a murder, you can handle this. Belly said you was the Black Sherlock Holmes."

"No, I'm not." Chelsea sighed. She just wanted to sweep up her broken glass and go home. She dropped the dustpan on the floor and began sweeping.

Lee Bee also left the kitchen and sat on the sofa with his friends.

Chelsea swept and felt like crap. This was a first. She had never been called over to solve a crime before. She didn't want to be a private detective. Especially not a pregnant one. Especially not a free one. She didn't even know these people. And she didn't have Snap or Carter to look out for her. This could go left and who would have her back?

"I'ma need yaw to empty your pockets and purses," Lee Bee announced to his friends to a mixed response. Si stood up and immediately started dropping items on the table. He grabbed his backpack from a hook by the door and dumped it on the table too. Mina and Trillness fussed in effrontery. Chelsea was accused again. But she just kept sweeping.

Until there was enough glass and dust in the pan. She took it to the garbage can in the kitchen. She glanced down into the trash and saw a stack of waffles. Everyone loved them. Who would throw them out? She tilted her head and considered the possibilities.

"Uggghhhh," she exhaled a deep and vexed sigh.
She knew what happened.

She went back into the living room as Mina was still protesting emptying her bag.

"If you my girl like you say you are, then this shouldn't be hard for you to do," Lee Bee stated in a raised voice.

"Nobody left out. So whoever took it is still in the room."

"That's not true, Lee. The mic isn't here," Chelsea said.

Lee Bee stood up. "You know who did it, Chelsea?"

"Yeah! She did it!" Mina yelled out. "Nothing else makes sense! You are accusing your friends and not this rat!"

"My brother is a detective. I could call him, and he could investigate this properly. Fingerprints and all that," Chelsea replied.

"Your brother will protect you! All I have to do is call Rashad, and he'll send his stepbrother over. He's very well-connected with the police," Mina bragged.

Chelsea chuckled again.

"I just want to know who stole from me. I don't want anybody to go to jail. No police, not your brother," he said looking at Chelsea, "or Rashad's stepbrother," he directed to Mina. "Same person, by the way!"

Chelsea laughed out. "I wanted to be the one to tell her."

"Wait! Are you Rashad's stepsister? He talks about you all the time," Mina said regretfully.

The worried look on her face was amusing to Chelsea. "I know."

Lee Bee was staring at Chelsea. She could feel his disappointment. But considering he was just using her for her brain, she didn't care if he was disappointed.

"Somebody in this room took my microphone! And nobody's leaving until I get it back!" he said defiantly. His door was remote controlled. He could probably lock them in if he wanted to keep them there. And they were seven stories up. So the window was out of the question.

"Aunt Simply left. I'm pretty sure your microphone was stashed in one of her leftover containers. The one with the waffles in it," Chelsea said very calmly.

"She trying to say Aunty did it?" Trillness was immediately offended. "Where you find this chick?"

But Lee Bee was still staring at Chelsea.

"I don't think she stole from you," Chelsea explained.

"She don't have to. There's nothing I wouldn't do for her," he said.

Chelsea nodded. "But, someone else could have dumped the waffles in the trash and put the mic in the container. She would've carried it out without knowing and probably put it straight in the fridge when she got home. You guys are all old friends. She wouldn't think twice letting that someone in for a meal, later on. That person could then retrieve the mic and eat some more good food."

Nobody liked Chelsea's version of the crime. There were sighs and hollerations.

"The drawer was closed before she left," Lee Bee said.

And that was true. Chelsea didn't notice it opened until 4:40.

"Well, that was probably to throw off the timeline and set me up. I'm not usually around when your things come up missing, right? All of this peeing makes me an easy fall guy." She was using bad jokes to cover her nervousness. She had never confronted anyone alone before.

"What things?" Si asked.

Lee Bee hesitated. "A lot of stuff been coming up missing lately."

"And I think Aunt Simply is unaware that she's been the one moving the missing items," Chelsea added.

The room got strangely quiet until Si broke the silence.

"So you wasn't gon' tell me somebody been stealing from you? I thought we was better than that?"

"At first I thought I was just losing stuff."

Chelsea could see in his face that Si was not satisfied with that answer.

"Like you said, we all have a relationship with Aunty. It could be anybody," Trillness said.

"Yeah. But you're the only one that helped her clean up today," Lee Bee yelled.

Chelsea was relieved that she didn't have to be the one to say it. "Awwww, Trill, tell me you didn't do this! We are a family," Mina cried out.

"Family? Right. The kind of family where we do all the work, and he gets all the money! If it wasn't for my YouTube channel, nobody would even know who Mag was! And he feeds me every now and then, and we supposed to be even?" Trillness screamed.

It took Si and Mina both their combined strengths to hold Lee Bee back from jumping on Trillness. The chubby vlogger hit the door remote and ran out of the loft as quickly as he could, yelling expletives on his way out. The scuffle had cost Mina the heel of her shoe.

The group plopped back onto the couch. Mina leaned forward and guzzled down the last of the champagne. No one said anything for about ten minutes. The only audible sound was that of Lee Bee's heavy breathing until Mina's phone chimed. She picked it up and read the text message.

"So, you only invited her here to catch one of us?" Her voice was calm and steely. Everyone was out of emotion.

"Why you say that?" Lee asked with the same stoic tone.

"Rashad sent a text. It says nobody fools Chelsea."

As the door was still open, Si stood up and walked out. He didn't even take his bag with him or any of the things he had spilled on the table. Mina limped behind him.

Lee Bee sighed. "I guess they mad at me."

"Can't say I blame them," Chelsea said. "There had to be a better way for you to figure this out without hurting your oldest friend, and her."

"I couldn't think of one."

"It's time for me to call an Uber."

Chelsea stood and picked up her purse. It would only take a couple of minutes for the car to come and longer for her to weave her way out of the old building.

"Why are you leaving?"

"My work is done. You only asked me over to help you. I can go now."

He stood up and put his arm around her waist. "That's not the only reason I invited you. It was part of the reason, but to be honest, I was feeling you even before I had this idea. I've never met anyone like you."

"I am pregnant, Lee. How is this happening?"

"You won't be pregnant forever. And you don't think a man can see beyond the belly? I wanted to get to know you. Am I wrong for that?"

Chelsea relaxed her tense posture. Lee Bee pulled her closer and kissed her gently on the lips. She liked it.

After Lee called Aunt Simply to catch her up on what happened, she had confirmed that the diamond mic was sealed in a plastic container mixed in between two waffles. He hung up and looked at Chelsea.

"What are we about to do?" he asked her boyishly.

"I could eat again but you gave away all the food. Guess you can take me to a restaurant. Lots of good ones around here."

"And then?"

Chelsea smiled at him, "I can't have sex with you, Lee. I hope you understand."

"It's cool, but you don't have to leave me. I had a rough day. I need a friend." He smiled back at her.

"Maybe you could tell me how a guy from Seven and Van Dyke ended up here?"

"You know, just because we were born on the block doesn't mean we have to stay there, physically or mentally. And if you like it there, that's cool. But don't let the zip code limit your mind."

"What about the other people that let my zip code limit me? Your friends thought I was a rat before I said a word."

He smacked his lips, "You can't worry about how people judge you before they know you. You show them better than you tell them. Just like you did today. What people think can't be the reason you do something or the reason you don't."

Chelsea nodded. He was right. It was time for her to stop letting other people's opinions mess with her mind.

"I like the hood," he said casually.

"I do too."

"I like my loft too."

"I do too."

"And there was a condo in Copenhagen that was sick!"

The two new friends laughed. He leaned in and smacked a quick kiss on her lips, and pulled her out of the door.

Chapter Thirty-two

"And why are we not going to your house?" a confused Lee Bee asked Chelsea after he pulled into the parking lot of Sam's Party Store. He had insisted on personally driving her home the next morning, although she told him she could make her way on her own.

"Snap and Car will ask too many questions. I'm not ready to answer. No one is going to believe that we went to sleep." She winked.

"But we're grown and consenting adults, right?" Lee Bee asked.

"In my family? No. Just drop me off here. This is fine. I live right down the street."

Lee Bee turned his face up but complied. He parked the Lexus truck, hopped out and ran around to the passenger side to open Chelsea's door. "For the record, I'm not feeling this. This is not how I treat women."

"Noted. I appreciate you letting me have my way." Chelsea looked up at him submissively. "I know you're probably thinking I'm lying about my living situation. I'm not."

Lee Bee gave an accepting nod. Chelsea could tell he was uncomfortable. She stepped up on her tippy toes and kissed his cheek. He grabbed her hand and clinched it. Her face still close to his, he leaned in for a kiss in the mouth. He wasn't greedy, just a couple of soft lip caresses before he released her.

"When can I see you again?" he asked.

"You're the busy world traveler. You tell me," she replied.

"Call me when you get home."

"Ok." She turned toward home, gave him a shy wave and began her slow stride down Plymouth Rd. She watched him pull out of the parking lot and zoom off toward the freeway. She felt a little giddy. It had been a while since she felt that exact swoon of new love. Only this time, it was followed immediately by new guilt.

She wouldn't lie to herself and say that she wasn't drawn to him when they had first met, or that running to the mall to buy new clothes wasn't in some way to impress him. But she honestly hadn't expected to stay with him the entire night, and open up to him, and establish emotional intimacy and kiss him over and over again. She was pregnant by another man. This was a very bad look.

The first time James had asked her out, she only accepted because he was cute and she was single. He treated her well, was respectful and employed. She was probably a little bored.

But she didn't meet too many men at Farmer Roger's. Mostly only married men came into the store. So going out with James became perfunctory. They established habits quickly. It took months before she told him about Madeleine's money. By then, she believed he understood her and wouldn't try to talk her into doing something she didn't want to do. Like drive the guilt car or spend the lottery winnings. And he didn't. Eventually, she trusted him. And her mother had always told her when love was right, it would be easy. James was easy.

But Lee Bee had penetrated her most staunch defenses in one night. And the last time a man broke through that quickly was five years ago, when a young lawyer made her fall in love with him, only to throw her away the second he realized that he couldn't turn her into a Gabrielle Union character.

Were her finely-tuned instincts failing her, or was Lee Bee just that wonderful?

The best man she knew was her father, Ray French. And even he had cheated on his wife and married his mistress. There was little hope that any man after that could do better. No, Lee Bee was probably not that wonderful. But someway, he had fooled Chelsea's sensors.

It only took one block for Chelsea to go from euphoric to disenchanted. She looked up at the sound of a lawnmower and Theodrick pushing it across his lawn.

"Hey, Beautiful." He turned off the mower. "Why you ain't come to my birthday party last weekend? It was lit. We shut Chuck's down."

Chelsea vaguely remembered seeing the invitation for Theodrick's party at Chuck's Millionaires Club on her Facebook news feed.

"I can't go out to the club like this," she answered him, pointing to her stomach.

"Snap came."

Chelsea wasn't surprised. Chuck's was a regular hangout for Snap and his homeboys. They had the best happy hour on the west side. Half-priced top shelf drinks and food until 8 PM. The whole neighborhood went straight from work.

"Glad you had fun. I'll try to come next year," Chelsea said.

"Well, start looking for a sitter now. I don't want to hear no excuses. You know I'm feeling you." He gave her the pervy up-and-down as usual.

"I got a man, Theodrick," she reminded him - and herself.

Maybe she had two.

"He locked up, Chelsea! You not gon' wait for him! You'll be old!"

"What about loyalty?"

"You gotta be loyal to you and your baby. You still young and fine. You got a couple good years left. Don't put your life on hold for James! You don't deserve that. You didn't kill nobody!" Theodrick said with conviction.

Chelsea smacked her lips. "Neither did James!"

Theodrick shook his head as if he pitied her. The same man that got fired from the car wash last year for washing the cars with the doors open was questioning Chelsea's logic and reasoning.

"Come on, Chels," he said before dismissing her with the ignition of his lawn mower. The powerful and loud engine would have drowned out any response that he obviously wasn't trying to hear.

She threw her hand at Theodrick and continued her walk of shame toward her house. She reached the corner that separated his block from hers. She was starting to dread facing Snap and having to explain why she hadn't come home from brunch until the following morning. The thought caused her to hesitate crossing the street.

A car that Chelsea didn't recognize was speeding up the side street. It was a red Camero with L'il Wayne screaming out of custom speakers. The driver had pulled up to Chelsea's feet in a weak effort to respect the stop sign. It was Lucien Fontaine, the youngest of the brothers. He had been living with the original clan in New Orleans, but Chelsea had gone to school with him once upon a time.

He pushed his sunglasses up to his forehead. He hadn't changed much in all these years. She still knew him.

"Careful, Luc," she said to him. "Don't hurt that pretty car."

"Heard you had one, too. A pretty car."

"Nothing like this," Chelsea said. "Besides, mine is previously owned."

"What you doing out here walking?" he asked.

"Complicated." She wasn't about to break down her family drama to a Fontaine. She was trying to figure out how he knew about her car. It never left the garage.

"Been a long time, Scooby," he teased, reminding her of her high school nickname. She smiled at him.

"Yeah, how have you been?"

"I been locked up. Just got out."

Not surprised, but knowing better than to say as much, she could only offer a "Welcome home."

His face tightened. "I missed my brother's funeral. I was on my way to his grave now. How about you come with me?"

"I can't, Luc. I have a Lamaze class," she lied. "But I was sorry to hear about Bou's death," she lied again.

"His murder. But you know that. Your brother caught the killer." His voice had gotten cold. She could feel his energy shifting as his sterile brown eyes stared right through her. "Heard he made detective and everything."

Chelsea nodded slowly. She and Luc had always gotten along. Never close friends but always friendly. The Fontaines didn't run in the same circles as Chelsea and Carter. Although Plymouth Road and Joy Road were only a mile apart, a lot happened in between that mile.

Of course, he would be upset about his brother's murder. But this conversation was taking a dark turn. And the look on his face was eerie and alarming.

"Well, you tell him how grateful I am that he located my brother's killer for me. Family is all a man really has. Worst feeling in the world is losing one of your own. Sure you don't want to go with me?"

Chelsea froze. She couldn't speak. She could barely shake her head.

"Maybe next time." He paused. Then he spoke deliberately, "Take care of that baby, Chelsea."

He pulled his sunglasses back over his eyes and sped down the street.

Chelsea could feel the tears welling up in her eyes. She blinked and took off walking as fast as her not-too-high heels would allow.

She could see Snap standing in his driveway. She burst into a run with tears fully streaming. He saw her running toward him. He dropped the water sprinkler he was holding and ran to meet her.

"What's wrong? Where have you been? Did Lee Bee do something to you?" He grabbed her, panicked.

She fell into his arms, sobbing. "Luc Fontaine," was all she could manage to get out. She was breathing heavy.

"Luc? What about him? He's down south." Snap knew two things Chelsea never did was run or cry. Seeing her do both freaked him out. "What the hell happened?!" he screamed.

She composed her tears and took a deep breath. Looking into her best friend's eyes, she said, "I think Luc Fontaine just threatened my baby!"

Chapter Thirty-three

Snap sat on his porch with a gun on his lap. It wasn't legally obtained. He'd bought it from a guy that was squatting in a house and selling all types of weapons of mass destruction out of the basement. It was a while back. Snap had forgotten he had the piece until Chelsea told him what Lucien Fontaine had said to her the day before.

Snap always trusted Chelsea's intuition and didn't believe that James was guilty. He had never given any thought to who might have actually killed Bou Fontaine. He didn't really care. The drama of James's arrest, Carter and Chelsea fighting all the time, and the pregnancy - it was all too much. Worrying over who killed Bou was the lowest of priorities. And maybe Chelsea was wrong. The Fontaines certainly thought so, or else they wouldn't have sent Luc to threaten Chelsea. And he was definitely sent. Everyone knew that Arcangelo Fontaine ran his family like Don Corleone. If Luc was back, it was for a reason. Running into Chelsea was not accidental.

The natural threat would have been toward James's sister, Denise, a sibling for a sibling. But Luc didn't come to Denise. He came to Chelsea, the keeper of the child, which made it evident to Snap which Fontaine was making the threat. Arcangelo.

"Don't tell Carter! He may do something stupid," Chelsea had pleaded with Snap earlier. She was right. Carter was likely to do something impulsive with the entire police department on his side, many of whom knew and despised the Fontaines. There would've been no shortage of officers willing to do whatever Carter asked.

Instead, she agreed to go to Boca Raton and spend some time with her father and his rich second wife. Chelsea must have been scared if she was seeking out the company of Miss Madeleine. Really scared. She had given Carter some crap story about Sapphire needing her help. He'd bought it.

So until she left, Snap sat a diligent watch on his front porch to make sure no one tried to get to Chelsea's house. She said she would leave for Florida in a day or so.

With all the commotion, he didn't get a chance to ask her why she had stayed out all night. Who was this Lee Bee character, anyway? Just some guy that goes to Spain with a rapper? That makes him sweet? He was skinny. Looked like he had never done a situp in his life. One thing about Chelsea, his dear friend knew how to pick a simple dude out from a mile away. Not that he was rooting for James, because he wasn't. He was a wrong guy long before any murder. But Snap had always figured that, when he was ready to settle down after he had all of his fun, he and Chelsea would just...

He sat up, alerted by a loud noise coming from Chelsea's backyard. He slowly stood as quietly as he could, hoping his porch steps wouldn't creak and give away his position. Taking the safety off the gun, he gently tiptoed down his front steps. Staying close to the house he crept up his driveway and moved toward his garage. He heard the noise again. Someone was definitely in Chelsea's backyard. Chelsea's bedroom was in the back of the house. Her window faced the backyard. Someone must have been trying to climb inside.

Snap ducked down low and crawled across his driveway to the fence that separated his and Chelsea's yards. He heard a boy's voice. "You too loud." Didn't sound more than seventeen. Had Arcangelo sent a child to harm Chelsea? Then he heard another voice from a young girl around the same age say, "I'm trying to get it open."

Snap was confused. He didn't know if he should start shooting or not. Then Chelsea's alarm system began to scream out. The entire backyard lit up like the Christmas tree at Rockefeller Center. His phone began to vibrate. It was Chelsea calling. Snap was staring at Chelsea's intruders. And they were staring back at him.

He answered the call.

"It's Olive and Kevin. I think they're trying to take your car," Snap said his voice trembling in the phone. She had obviously tripped a sensor. "Damn it, Olive! I almost shot you!"

The alarm system that Ray had installed in the house shortly before moving to Boca Raton was programmed to alert Carter if it activated. So within two minutes of receiving the alert, Carter was calling Chelsea. She had by this time come into the backyard.

Chelsea deactivated the alarm, but not before several neighbors came out, standing on their porches. She was barefoot in the grass when she answered his FaceTime.

"Calm down, Car, I'm okay. Ollie and Kev tried to take my car."

Carter laughed out loud. "Senior summer picnic is tonight."

It wasn't funny. But Carter didn't know why, and Chelsea wasn't about to tell him. She looked at Snap who was shaking and pacing up and down his driveway, and then back at Olive who had the good sense to be quiet. Kevin just kept apologizing.

"Well, at least we know the alarm works. Good night, Carter," Chelsea said, walking across the grass and up the back steps. "Olive, I want my car keys back."

She went inside her house and slammed the door.

"Is she mad?" Kevin asked sheepishly.

"She ain't mad. I told you she wasn't gon' trip," Olive said defiantly with her lips poked out.

"I am!" Snap's stony face let Olive know that he meant business. He couldn't tell Olive exactly why what she did was so wrong. After all, a few days before and Chelsea would've just fussed at the teenagers and called Aunt Grace.

But he knew how scared she was, how scared he was.

"Get yaw little asses out of here." He watched Olive's face turn from defiant to concerned.

"What's going on, Snap?" She handed him Chelsea's car keys. "You just tried to steal a car, scared your pregnant cousin, and almost got shot! What do you think is going on?" he yelled back at Olive.

Olive's eyes welled up with tears. Snap and Olive had never exchanged harsh words before.

"We're sorry," Kevin said. "Let's just go, Ollie." He pulled his girlfriend out the backyard. Snap watched them walk down the driveway.

Chelsea opened the back door and stepped out onto the back porch. "Are they gone?"

Snap nodded.

Chelsea sighed.

"What are you gonna do about them?" Snap asked angrily. "They need them little asses beat."

"I'll tell Daddy. He'll handle Ollie. I don't have the energy."

"I'll do it. I don't think I've ever been this pissed off at kids in my life!" Snap kept replaying the moment he had hesitated firing the gun.

"Give me the gun, Devin," Chelsea said calmly. She stepped off the porch and onto the grass. Snap walked to her and handed her his illegal weapon.

"I'm sorry. I just wanted to..." His voice cracked.

"I know. You got me. And I got you." She turned around and went back up the steps. "Tell you what, keep the keys. You can drive the car while I'm gone. But only at night."

Snap smiled. "Needs a car wash. I'll take care of it."

"You always take care of everything. That's why I love you," Chelsea said as she stepped back into the house.

"I love you too, Chelsea," Snap said to himself. He stood and waited for her motion lights to go out. In the darkness, he smacked himself in the head for buying that gun.

Chapter Thirty-four

Young Maddy Baker had to drop out of high school after she got knocked up at sixteen. In those days, pregnant teens weren't allowed to go to high school, so she had to go at night to the Stevenson Building on Grand River Avenue where she received her GED and regular doses of shame.

It wasn't easy to find work as a teen mom with little education, but Maddy eventually got hired to clean the house of the Morgan family. They lived in Birmingham, a wealthy suburb several miles north of Detroit. Maddy didn't have a car, so after dropping Diamondique off at the neighborhood daycare center, she would take the Clairmont bus to Woodward, then transfer to the Woodward bus that would take her to Eight Mile. Detroit City buses don't run in the suburbs, so from there she had to get a SEMTA bus to take her from Eight Mile to Maple Avenue in Birmingham. She walked a mile and a half from there.

The Morgans were good people. The husband, William, was a financial advisor, and his wife, Elizabeth, stayed at home, barely took care of the children, and did charity work when she wasn't drunk at the country club. Maddy worked hard and had even picked Miss Elizabeth up off the floor a few times and put her to bed before her husband came home. She took excellent care of the Morgan children, and Miss Elizabeth appreciated that, given her general lack of interest in them. She began to give Maddy her daughter's old hand-me-downs, all of which were expensive brands. Diamondique was the best-dressed toddler in her daycare. Mr. Morgan had grown especially fond of Maddy after coming home early one day to find that she had put Miss Elizabeth to bed around 3 PM, cleaned the house, started dinner and was helping their oldest son with his homework while playing dolls with the youngest daughter. The previous maids had all quit because of Elizabeth's drinking. But Maddy seemed to roll with it just fine. As thanks, Mr. Morgan gave Maddy his old Jeep Wrangler so that she wouldn't have to catch the bus anymore.

Maddy worked for the Morgans for five happy years, seeing the oldest through high school and the youngest to fourth grade. She had come to have great affection for the family, and they seemed to have affection for her. One day, Mr. Morgan came home and announced that the family would be moving to Boca Raton. His business was doing well, and there were many wealthy retirees there for him to make even more money managing their accounts. By the end of the month, the Morgans had moved, and Maddy was out of a job. Mr. Morgan had given her a generous severance package, a letter of recommendation, and a promise that if she ever came to Florida, they would make a place for her.

After 34 years of playing the daily three digit, four digit, and weekly Big Game, Maddy moved to Florida. Boca Raton, in fact, and insisted on being called Miss Madeleine. It didn't take her long to track down the Morgan family. She wanted them to see her at her best, to know that she had made it. She found the family a fractured version of what they once were. Mr. Morgan had died on the golf course ten years before, the oldest child in and out of rehab, and the youngest living in Israel. Miss Elizabeth was older and drunker, sitting on the lanai of her beachfront home, barely remembering Maddy and having little interest in getting to know Miss Madeleine. She came every week to sit and talk with her anyway. She had been promised a place.

"My stepdaughter, Chelsea, is coming into town today. We're throwing her a baby shower this weekend," Madeleine said, sipping bourbon and lemonade, a drink Miss Elizabeth had invented forty years ago.

"Is that the nasty one?" Miss Elizabeth asked.

"Yes, that's her. I just know she's going to find something wrong with this party. She hates everything I do. Lord knows, I try for that girl. And it's never good enough," Madeleine whined.

"Her mother should have slapped you across the face." Miss Elizabeth sipped her own bourbon and lemonade. "Back in '87, my William cheated on me with some whore from his office. I confronted her and slapped her across the face six, maybe seven times, until her face was red and my hand ached. He bought me a new Jag the next day, and we never spoke of it again."

Miss Elizabeth's moments of clarity were few and far between. It wasn't always easy to tell when she was lucid or just babbling.

"Well, don't you see?" Miss Elizabeth continued. "Her mother never confronted you. She never got the chance to give you a good slappin'. And so the daughter hates you. You could easily fix this."

"How?" Madeleine inquired.

"By letting the little cow hit you, dear. Six, maybe seven times. How can you not see that?"

Miss Madeleine stood up. "Would you like to come to the shower? I can send a car for you. It would do you good to get out of the house."

Miss Elizabeth turned her face up. "No, but you can send me some of your delicious fried chicken. You know I always loved it."

Madeleine smiled. Sometimes Miss Elizabeth did remember those years when Maddy was her girl.

"I have caterers, darling." Madeleine had picked up her purse from the table and turned to leave.

"Maddy, dear, do me a favor and pick up Candace from school today. I have a headache from all this lemonade. She gets embarrassed when I have my headaches."

"Yes, Miss Elizabeth," Madeleine said as she walked off the lanai to the driveway and got into her Mercedes.

Chapter Thirty-five

It really could have been a beautiful, modern, nine-bedroom mansion if Maddy had hired a real interior designer instead of letting her cousin do it.

The contractors were still regularly at the Baker-French Mansion. Sometimes it seemed that the house would never be finished. Adding chrome to this door, brass to that molding, a chandelier in the other room, or whatever gaudy accessory Maddy came across watching design TV shows. The pool area had an Egyptian theme, except for the jacuzzi that was shaped like a margarita glass. The bathrooms were Grecian with frescos of Zeus on the ceiling looking down over the toilets.

The bedrooms were styled after African royalty, something like the Eddie Murphy classic, Coming To America. Every bedroom had a patio adorned with an African statue, genitals to scale. Carter had refused to sleep in one room during his first visit.

"As a man, I can not sleep in a room with a naked dude staring back at me." He elected instead to sleep in a deck chair by the pool underneath a gilded fountain in the shape of an Egyptian arm. The next day, Maddy had the statue removed and replaced with a topless African woman carrying a basket on her head. Breasts to scale. Carter moved back into the bedroom.

Most recently, one whole side of the mansion had been remodeled to provide access for Madeleine's mother, Poochie, in her customized scooter. Now she could drain the battery zooming around the house. Poochie hated sitting idly for too long. The ramps gave her more freedom and Madeleine more peace.

For Chelsea, the best part of the estate was the small carriage house behind the garage. Close enough, but far enough away. The original owners had intended it for staff, live-in maids, home health workers, or the chauffeur. But Madeleine didn't want any woman younger or more attractive than her living with her husband. So she didn't allow live-in staff. The women that worked for Miss Madeleine went home to their own beds at the end of the workday. So it was always free for Chelsea's visits. It was about the size of one of the master bedrooms with a sitting area and dinette set, small microwave and mounted television. It was the only part of the estate that hadn't been remodeled. It was perfect.

But first, Chelsea had to get through the main house.

Diamondique, considering herself the family fashionista, had purchased a custom-made Louis Vuitton sofa, loveseat and recliner for the living room and was sitting with her feet up when Chelsea walked in and dropped her luggage.

"Well, I'm here," Chelsea said unemotionally.

Diamondique stood, walked over and gave Chelsia a less-than-enthusiastic hug.

"Hey, girl. It's about time you dragged your butt down here. We see your daddy more than you do," she said as she sauntered her wide hips back to the easy chair.

Chelsea could think of three or four different comebacks to that crack, mostly revolving around the fact that their mother had stolen her father from his actual family. But instead, she smiled and said, "I'm very busy, and this pregnancy doesn't give me a lot of energy."

Sapphire ran into the room. She had an hourglass figure that jumped in all the right places when she ran, and long Havana twists to throw off of her shoulder before grabbing Chelsea.

"I'm so glad you're finally here! We're going to have such a great time!" She was hugging Chelsea vigorously. "I can't wait to tell you about my new boyfriend." Sapphire always told Chelsea about her boyfriends.

"What new boyfriend?" Diamondique asked, confused.

Miss Madeleine and Ray came walking in from the patio. He released himself from the tight grip of his rich second wife's hand long enough to embrace his daughter and kiss her forehead.

"How are you, Baby Girl? I've missed you."

Miss Madeleine followed with much less effort of the same gesture, their bodies never touching. It was more of a leaning that didn't quite connect.

"Chelsea, dear, don't make any plans for the weekend. We have a surprise for you," she said.

"Oh I know, you're throwing me a baby shower."

The dejected looks on Sapphire's and Diamondique's faces let Chelsea know she wasn't supposed to know. "Oh, come on, Sapph. You didn't really think I believed Di needed me to help with her store inventory, did you?"

Back in the old days, Diamondique sold fake purses at the swap meet. But today, she owned three boutiques in Florida where she sold handbags, shoes, and jewelry. Mostly all of it real. "Well, can you at least pretend to be surprised?" Sapphire asked.

"No, let's just get through it."

The room became awkwardly quiet. Chelsea looked down at her luggage then back up at her father.

"Daddy, can you help me carry these to the carriage house, please?" she asked like a polite ten-year-old right before a curtsy.

"We were hoping you'd stay in the house with us this time. You're pretty far along, and if something were to happen, you might need us near you," Maddy said.

Chelsea pretended to deliberate, then said, "The carriage house is fine." Waking up in the night and seeing a naked statue might send her into early labor.

"Carter told me that you helped him with another one of his cases," Ray said, obviously trying to change the subject.

"Yeah. I was waiting until I saw you to tell you the whole story. Me, Snap and Rashad went to this studio because somebody wants to buy a record label." She winked at her father, knowing he would get her sarcasm.

"A record label? Rashad told me he was donating money to some music teachers!" Maddy interrupted.

Chelsea ignored Maddy and sat down. She told her father the whole story of the murder, the Totty confrontation, and even how she went to Lee Bee's house and found who'd stolen his property. Fearing her father's temper, she left out the part where she had spent the night with him. And the Luc Fontaine epilogue.

"How come Rashad didn't get to go to the hip-hop brunch? What? They think they better than him?" Diamondique asked with an offended tone.

"They're actually in hip-hop, Rashad isn't. Lee Bee manages artists and goes all over the world doing concerts. He's a professional."

Rashad, on the other hand, was begging to hand a bag of money over to a murderer. A small point that Chelsea withheld from his mother as a favor.

"You like him," Sapphire observed rather accurately. "I can tell by the way you're talking about him."

"He's cool."

"You were smiling the whole time you were talking about him. And you never smile."

"I always smile!" Chelsea yelled with a frown on her face.

"Is he cute?" Diamondique asked.

"Gorgeous," Chelsea said, smiling again.

"There it is!" Sapphire was laughing and pointing at Chelsea's face. "You like him! Come on, let's go to the carriage house, and you can tell me all about him."

Chelsea giggled like a teenager.

"Chelsea, who is the baby daddy?" Maddy asked calmly. "I keep feeling like you lying to us about the parentage. Something is not adding up."

"What? Are we back on this again?" Chelsea snapped back at Maddy. "It ain't even none of your business."

Maddy sighed. "I told you she was lying to us, Ray."

"Ain't nobody lying to you! Who are you that I gotta lie to? I already told you this is James's baby!"

"I think it's odd that you would be pregnant by one man, engaged to another man, and having brunch with a third man. You might as well tell us. We're gonna find out in a few weeks when we see the baby's face. Babies always look just like their daddies when they're born," Maddy said.

"Down south, they say the baby is always born looking like whoever worried the mother the most when she was pregnant," Sapphire added.

"Well, if that's the case, Babe is gonna look like yaw!" Chelsea quipped.

"Oh, my Lord! Is Rashad the baby daddy? That's incest!" Maddy screamed out with an overdramatic demi-faint.

"No, it's not! And he ain't related to me!"

"Chelsea! Are you sleeping with Rashad?" Ray had grabbed her by the forearms like he did when he caught her trying to sneak out to the Pretty Ricky concert when she was sixteen.

"No, Daddy! Let me go," she protested.

"Double Aunties!" Sapphire was saying in the background.

Chelsea broke away from her father and pulled back.

"Everybody, quiet! Listen to me! This is James' baby. Not Snap's, not Lee Bee's, and definitely not Rashad's. My life is not a soap opera. Don't nobody say nothing else to me!"

With a slight teeter, she grabbed all her bags on her own and began to struggle out of the room. The sooner she could get to the carriage house and pretend she was somewhere else, the better.

She could hear Maddy saying, "After I put that new statue of the African queen giving birth into that room..."

Chelsea didn't even look back. She just moved her bags out of the patio door, up a side trail that led to the driveway, which wound around the garage and led to the carriage house. As soon as she got to the driveway, she heard the familiar stride of her father's footsteps coming up behind her. He took her carry-on bag and slung it over his shoulder. He moved her hand away from the handles of her two roll-aways and paced himself beside her.

"I'm your father. It's my job to care about who you are making babies with," he said softly.

"But it's not your job to run away with every crazy thought she puts into your head. You do know me, right?" Chelsea replied, albeit keeping her tone respectful.

"Yeah, but you know Miss Madeleine's family is wild like that. Half her cousins don't know who their fathers are. She just used to drama. I'm sorry. I believe you."

They reached the outside of the small carriage house.

Chelsea looked at her father. "Daddy, do I have to do this baby shower? I just know it's going to be awful."

"It would make me so happy if you did. You're so independent. Let us do this one thing for you."

Chelsea sighed. "Okay."

She turned to open the door, and he stopped her. "There's just a couple of things you should know first."

"What?" Chelsea asked.

Ray hesitated for a second before answering. "Poochie's coming."

"Makes sense. That's Maddy's momma, and she lives here." Chelsea shrugged.

"And Crystal."

Chelsea shrugged again. Crystal was probably the loudest woman in Detroit. She used to come into the store. Chelsea would be way back in frozen foods and could hear her talking at the register. But she was okay, as far as Chelsea was concerned. Could've been worse. Could've been...

"And Charles."

Maddy's youngest brother, Charles. He had it in his head that he and Chelsea had a romantic future. He used to come into the store too, to harass Chelsea and scare off anyone he thought was interested. Once he had caught James in the parking lot bringing Chelsea flowers. He had lied and told James that she was in a produce meeting and had offered to give her the flowers. When Charles came inside, he presented them to Chelsea as his own gift. Of course, Chelsea was annoyed that James had believed there was such thing as a "produce meeting."

"So basically, there will be more of Maddy's family at my baby shower than my own?" Chelsea asked.

"Grace and Olive are flying in," Ray said, like it was a consolation prize. "You don't really have any girlfriends."

Chelsea hadn't yet told her father about Olive's attempted heist.

Ray made Chelsea promise to take a nap before seeing the family. He had hoped a little rest might find her in a better mood at dinner. Little did he know, she had no intention of coming back to the main house for dinner. She would be saving her strength for the impending, unavoidable and calamitous baby shower.

She spent the rest of the week in bed. The third trimester had brought a lot of physical exhaustion and achiness. Babe was kicking mercilessly, poking vital organs and interrupting sleep. The fatigue was real, and the charlie horses were excruciating—but also a useful excuse for avoiding Ray's other family. He came to sit with her regularly. He had a list of baby names he wanted her to consider. All of them included Raymond.

The morning of the baby shower, Chelsea was startled out of her sleep by the landscaper's very big and very loud lawn mowers. She had breakfast in bed for the fourth day in a row and watched television for another hour before getting up. She showered and rubbed shea butter on her stomach, breasts, and booty to reduce the postnatal stretchmarks that she feared more than a world war. She didn't want her body looking tired and worn out at only 28. What if no man thought she was attractive anymore? What if there was something to her chemistry with Lee Bee? He was very respectful the other night, but eventually, he would want to see her undressed.

Granted, when she first began to have concerns, it was more about what James would think of her body after birth. But, it had been hard to cope these last few months. James hadn't been writing or even calling. If Chelsea wanted to make her peace with the fact James was gone, she would have to distance him in her mind. Of course, that's what was making it so easy for someone like Lee Bee to creep in. That, and the fact he was the most fascinating man she had ever met.

Yes, Romeo was an impressive man, definitely a good look for a girl from the block. He was handsome, smart, and Black enough. But he was also educated and polished in many ways that Chelsea was not. Meanwhile, Lee Bee was just like Chelsea. A child of the ghetto, rough around the edges and still real. Sapphire was right. Chelsea did like him.

She decided to call him, finally. He seemed fairly annoyed with the way she had left town abruptly without even a text message.

"I mean, if you got yourself into some trouble, you could tell me. You did help me out. I owe you." He had tried to understand her impulsive decision to relocate indefinitely.

But she couldn't tell him. Or Carter. Or Ray. Not yet. Keeping the baby safe was her number one concern. And as much as she hated Boca Raton, it was the last place anyone would expect her to be.

Then she called Snap.

"I told a couple of the neighbors that you went to Arizona to have the baby with your mom's family."

Leave it to Snap to send the bloodhounds in the opposite direction. He was smart like that. Chelsea told him all about the baby shower she didn't want, and Charles.

"Charles got you pinned up in that house. He might wear you down," he teased.

"Every time he comes near me I'm gon' fake a contraction," Chelsea said.

Last, she called Carter, who made her promise to send as much video and photo footage as she could. Not because he wanted to share his sister's big day, but because he wanted to laugh at Maddy's ghetto family.

She dropped the phone on the bed and sighed when she caught a glimpse of herself in the mirror. Her hair was a mess. She hadn't been combing it. Four days of buns, gels and edge control had taken their toll. She released the last bobby pin from her hair, and it didn't move like it was stuck up there. Was this sham of a shower even worth what she was sure would be a painful detangling?

She could hear her mother's voice advising her on the situation: "Baby Girl, just because you don't want to go somewhere doesn't mean you shouldn't be fine when you get there. Almost everything is boring after an hour or so. Looking good is the only real reason to go anywhere."

Chelsea nodded in the mirror. Diane was right. One day, Babe would see the pictures of this day, and he would be proud of how good his mom looked at 33 weeks.

"Okay, I'll do my hair." The baby kicked a few times as if to say, "Thank you."

Three hours later, Chelsea was struggling into a sunset orange maxi dress that fit all of her curves in the back and had ample room in the front for her biggest curve. She was determined to be sexy preggers and not homely preggers. Even if it meant wrestling with the dress that should have had a zipper.

Ray knocked twice before opening her door. "Baby Girl, the guests are starting to arrive. You can't be late for your own shower." He gazed at her and stopped. "You look just like your mother when she was pregnant with Carter. Same hair, same disgusted look on her face."

Chelsea laughed. Ray often told her how much she made faces like her mother. And she wore her hair in one of Diane's signature styles. If her mother couldn't be at the shower, at least her swag could be.

Chelsea slid her mildly swollen feet into a pair of black BeBe platform flip-flops. Her feet were fat but pretty, no reason not to show them. Her father took her by the arm and walked her over to the main house. She could see through the windows that the caterers were putting the finishing touches on a buffet laid out in the dining room. Diamondique and Sapphire were leveling a banner on the wall. Chelsea smiled.

"This is nice."

"Yes," Ray said. "Hopefully you will be too."

"No promises," she said, laughing. Ray also laughed. He knew she was a stinker, but when Maddy wasn't around, he found it amusing.

As father and daughter walked past the golden sphinx that sat across from the pool toward the patio door, Maddy came out also wearing an orange dress. Chelsea furrowed her brow and walked past her into the house.

"Look, Chelsea, we both wearing orange. We could be twins," Maddy said as Chelsea passed.

"In what carnival mirror?" Chelsea quickly retorted.

Diamondique rushed over to Chelsea and ushered her into the living room, where some of the guests had begun to arrive. Chelsea didn't know any of them, but she didn't expect that she would. She smiled politely and mentally prepared herself for the next few hours of boring conversation.

But no one attempted any. She plopped on the couch because it was the only way she could sit these days, crossing her legs at the ankle and looking up at the three older ladies sitting across from her. They were staring sternly and had shook their heads. Chelsea pulled her phone out of the pocket of her maxi dress.

"Can I get a pic of you ladies? My brother wants me to send him as many as I can," she asked. The ladies offered an obliging smile and leaned in for Chelsea's picture.

She sent it to Carter with a caption. These old birds keep mean mugging me.

Carter immediately texted back about 35 emojis, all laughing.

"Any luck finding the father, dear?" one of the older women asked.

An hour later, the shower was in full swing. Diamondique and Sapphire had done a wonderful job decorating. Madeleine and her sister, Crystal, were doing great hosting the dozens of people that had come, some of them even bringing gifts. Others brought prayers for Chelsea's plight into single motherhood. They were members of Madeleine's new church and had come to see the mansion and eat for free. A fact Olive questioned loudly.

"Why is they here?" she kept asking.

Madeleine explained. "Chelsea doesn't have any friends. If it weren't for my church, we could have had this shower over the phone."

Chelsea wasn't the only one confused by the guest list.

Poochie was zooming around the pool inspecting plates and counting servings. Then she would come back and report to Chelsea.

"Some of these folks done had three plates and ain't even came to say hello to you."

Chelsea was grateful for those that had obviously only come to eat and revel. At least they weren't asking awkward personal questions about her child's father. Madeleine had painted quite the forlorn picture of Chelsea to her church brethren.

Crystal had dressed to match the thematic colors of the shower: white and gold. She had just gotten her DNA results back from Ancestry.com and, after learning of her Ivorian heritage, had decided to immerse herself in the culture. That also explained why the colors for the shower had been changed from baby blue and white. It was also why the Pandora radio was playing drums softly in the background.

The food was excellent. Whoever these caterers were, they knew what they were doing. Chelsea found the deliciousness of the provisions to be the best distraction of the day. She was at the buffet table for the fourth time when Olive approached her, sulking. Chelsea put her plate down and opened her arms for embrace. Olive hugged Chelsea. "I'm sorry. I was wrong. Can you please talk to me again?"

"Of course, Baby Cuz," Chelsea said. She could never stay mad at Olive for long. "You have to call Snap and apologize too. You really scared him."

Olive nodded.

"Did you try the crab cakes?" Chelsea asked, handing Olive a plate. She was glad they were talking again. There was no one else in the room Chelsea could crack jokes with.

As Olive took the plate and began piling on the shrimp scampi, a woman approached Chelsea.

"You know that Moses's real momma gave him away so that he could have a better life?" the strange woman said.

"Are you suggesting I put my baby in the river?" Chelsea asked.

"Look how good he turned out," the woman replied.

"He was raised rich and chosen by God. Of course he turned out good."

There had been a few weird bible conversations like this one. Someone earlier had scolded her for not waiting for Boaz. Before she could formulate a clap back, Charles stepped up.

"Who is Boaz? He from Detroit? That's your new man?" He was speaking as if he had caught her having an affair.

Chelsea sighed. "I'm so mad I can't run."

"That should be my baby."

"But I can still hit you with this plate!" she barked at him.

He grabbed her by her arm.

"I'm telling my Daddy!" she threatened. He let her go.

Chelsea already knew that Charles didn't want to spar with Ray French.

"I'm just playin' with you, Goofy!" he said, walking away quickly.

After Chelsea and Olive had finished eating, they drifted out to the pool area. Maddy and some of the other guests were surrounding a man Chelsea didn't know. Since Chelsea had refused to play any shower games, there was an obvious lull in the festivities. And this man seemed to be filling the void with charismatic banter.

"In Foz do Iguaçu, we were able to feed many children and we even helped build a school," he was saying as Chelsea approached the group. She threw her eyebrows up. Another one of Maddy's church friends.

"Chelsea!" Maddy called out. "This is Pastor DeWylin. He and his wife came to bless your baby."
"Maybe later," Chelsea mouthed sardonically.

"It's a pleasure to meet you, Chelsea," Pastor DeWylin said with a kind face. "I was just telling everyone about my recent trip to Brazil. My wife and I do a lot of missionary work there. Maybe if you're free this week, you can come to the church and help us make care packages for our next trip."

"Perhaps." Chelsea shrugged.

"It'll help you take your mind off all your own problems," a random voice spoke out.

"Finish telling us about the trip," another one of the ladies said loudly.

"Well," Pastor had started to snicker. "My wife had a hard time with the language."

He continued to laugh, and a tall, slender woman swooped her long red ponytail across her shoulder. "What can I say? I studied French in high school. I tried the Rosetta Stone on the plane, but my Spanish was awful. Caballo means horse, but cabello means hair. I kept saying I wanted to wash my horse."

Everyone laughed. Chelsea decided she didn't like the Pastor and turned to walk back into the house. Olive followed her.

"When can we cut my cake?"

"It's in the kitchen," Olive replied.

Chelsea and Olive headed to find cake and noticed Poochie, Crystal and an old white lady sitting quietly in the den entrenched in something on the television. She wandered toward them and Crystal had to scoot over on the sectional to make room for her.

"What's going on?" Chelsea asked.

"Law and Order marathon," Poochie said. "I only watch the S. Epatha Merkerson episodes. Baddest chick on TV!"

"Cain't nobody do it like Van Buren!" Crystal seconded.

"You know she was from Detroit?" the white woman added.

"Tell me how she never got an Emmy for this!" Poochie said. "Racism in Hollywood. What else? If she looked like the Good Wife she'd have a hundred awards!"

Chelsea sat next to Crystal. "I didn't know you were such a fan."

"Aren't you?"

"I like SVU."

"You got to watch regular Law and Order. It's the best one. Once I beat a ticket in court talking like Sam Waterson." Chelsea nodded. The ladies watched in silence until Chelsea remembered that she had wanted dessert. "I need cake." She nudged at Olive.

"Sit, little mother. My girl, Maddy, will go get you whatever you want," the older woman suggested. "Maddy! Maddy!"

Poochie turned to give a menacing look to the older woman. "Umm, Elizabeth! Maddy don't work for you no more!"

"She doesn't mind," Elizabeth protested. "She's very helpful. Where's my girl?"

Sapphire, who looked the most like her mother, walked into the room. She was bringing her grandmother a bottle of beer."

"Oh, there you are Maddy. Our little mother wants cake. Be a dear." Elizabeth threw her hand up and waived Sapphire away.

Crystal poked her lips. "Maddy need to come get her."

"She's on the patio with the pastor," Chelsea offered.

"I cain't hear S. Epatha!" Poochie yelled out.

Crystal's face perked up. "Pastor's here? Maddy is making a big donation to his new church." She stood up and fixed her dress. "I need my name on this too."

What was it about this family giving money to charlatans? Chelsea exhaled loudly and tapped Olive's shoulder. "Go get Daddy. And find me some cake!"

Chapter Thirty-six

Chelsea and Carter had always been Diane's children. They were both so like her. Ray French missed his first wife but still saw her in Carter's temper and Chelsea's impatience. And the facial expressions. Like her mother, Chelsea could make a face that read like an essay. And he couldn't admit it to Maddy, but sometimes Carter would smile, and the reminder of Diane's dimple would sadden him for the rest of the day.

Diane was methodical and savvy. It wasn't easy cheating on her. She knew his patterns and habits and noticed immediately when they had started to change. But she didn't say anything to him. He thought she was distracted and used it to spend more time with Maddy. For about a year, he had believed that he was fooling her.

One evening, he came home to find his children distraught. Diane had collapsed earlier and they had just returned home from the emergency room. Carter had tried several times to reach Ray, but his phone kept going directly to voicemail.

Ray had turned his phone off because he was with Maddy and she hated when his family called. Naturally, he had lied to his children and blamed his absence on a broken phone. Carter believed him. Ray was pretty sure that Chelsea did not.

It was that evening when his wife admitted to him that she had found a lump in her breast that had been diagnosed as malignant weeks before. She didn't want to tell the children right away, but after Ray's no-show at the hospital, she made it clear that whatever he was doing on the side needed to stop. That's when he found out that she had known all along. And he complied with his dying wife's request. In spite of his attraction to Maddy, he loved Diane.

Although Diane never discussed what she knew about Maddy with either of her children, Chelsea had figured out most of it on her own. But her mother's illness had absorbed much of her time and energy. She had actually stopped talking to Ray for a while. And whenever he lied to her or Carter about where he was going, she would tilt her head.

The last four years had been strained between Ray and his only daughter. It was like she had been stuck in the anger phase of grief. He tried to be patient with her. He pulled back and didn't smother her. He rarely mentioned career or marriage. He offered to buy her a house but she declined, due to her attachment to her late mother. He picked his battles, the main reason he had allowed her to stay in the ghetto. Then he looked up one day, and she was pregnant by a convicted felon. He blamed himself, of course, for moving away from her. But he was determined to be there for her now, whether she liked it or not. He was looking forward to being the number-one grandfather. He had already bought a hat that said so.

He snuck into the carriage house for some privacy, something he did often. He had snagged a plate from the buffet and was enjoying an episode of Law and Order when Olive opened the door, looking for him.

"What is it, Ollie?" he asked, slightly annoyed. Maddy allowed him so very little alone time.

"Uncle Ray, Chelsea told me to come get you. She in the house."

Ray feared she was fighting with Maddy. The two were always on the verge. He moved quickly back to the house.

He walked past his wife with her sister and pastor friend by the pool. Ray wasn't terribly fond of that guy. DeWylin was too doting on Maddy. But he appreciated the distraction it gave her. He saw Chelsea, who was beckoning him to come into the sitting room. He walked toward her, dreading whatever was about to happen. Between Poochie's mouth and Miss Elizabeth's dementia, it couldn't be good.

"Daddy, you can't let your wife give that pastor any money."

"You blocking the TV, Ray!" Poochie screamed out. Ray stepped closer to Chelsea.

"She loves that guy. He told her he would name an orphanage after her."

"I seriously doubt there's a church or an orphanage."

"What?"

Charles had wandered in with a plate in hand stuffing his face, as he always seemed to be doing.

"Found out who Boaz is. It's me!" he said to Chelsea.

"Charles! If you don't get outta here interrupting my TV, it's gon' be a funeral instead of a baby shower! In fact, everybody get out!" Poochie was yelling. Charles immediately ducked back out of the room. Ray and Chelsea followed suit.

"This is my house, dear," Miss Elizabeth said to Poochie. "See yourself out."

Ray sighed, knowing he would have to deal with these dueling old ladies soon. "What are you saying, Baby?"

"They don't speak Spanish in Brazil, Daddy. They speak Portuguese."

Olive held a plate with a giant piece of cake out to Chelsea, who smiled when she saw it. "Thanks, Baby Cuz."

Ray didn't fully understand the importance of what she had said. He had hoped that Maddy would.

Chapter Thirty-seven

Chelsea had decided that she had enough of the shower. She told Sapphire that her back and legs were hurting before taking another plate back to the carriage house.

She laid across the bed, sucking on a crab leg, and heard a light rap at the door.

She sighed and wiggled into a sit up position. "Charles."

The door opened and Maddy dipped her head in. "Mind if I come in? I brought more cake."

Chelsea waved her in.

Maddy had placed a mound of cake on the small dinette table. "You know, Chelsea dear, I am Rashad's mother, but I am not Rashad."

"What does that mean?"

"I only invited the pastor so you could feel him out." She smiled as she walked back to the door.

"Really?"

"I was your manager for five years. I remember when you were the only one to figure out that the Little Debbie's delivery driver was conning Mr. Ali."

Chelsea remembered that. He was padding the order and pocketing the change from cash payments.

"DeWylin was good," Maddy continued, "covered all his bases. I knew if he tripped up it would be something small that everyone would miss but you. Like Portuguese."

"And you wanted him to bless my baby?"

Maddy laughed. "I knew you would never go for that."

"What are you gonna do now?"

"Nothing. I'm not about to judge him or accuse him of anything. He just ain't gettin' my money."

She closed the door behind her.

Chelsea fell back on the bed and returned to the Law and Order marathon. S. Epatha Merkerson was talking to Jesse L. Martin in the final scene. She said, "You know, I used to wake up in the morning, brush my teeth, comb my hair, look in the mirror, and see a cop looking back at me. Now I got six eyes looking back. A cop, a black woman, a mother."

"That's real," Chelsea said to herself.

Chapter Thirty-eight

Romeo accepted payment in kind. Many of his clients were too poor to pay his fees traditionally but would compensate him with free meals, and old clothing. Like the peacoat Mrs. Wilder had given him after he had represented her grandson, Malcolm. It had belonged to her husband when he was a sailor in the '70s. Now, it was perfectly vintage and presently Romeo's favorite coat. Then there was the cherrywood armoire that Gregory Phillips had given him, even though Romeo was unable to prevent Philips's daughter from being convicted of aiding and abetting her drug dealing boyfriend.

When Grandmother Phillips had passed away a year later, Gregory invited Romeo to take his pick of her furniture before he gave the rest to the Salvation Army. Romeo only went to the house as a kindness, not expecting to find more than the typical plastic covered crap. The cherrywood armoire and matching trunk were handcrafted and had been in the family for decades.

Romeo was so enamored with the pieces, he insisted on giving Gregory $300 for the set. He called his father to help him move the furniture, who, upon seeing the armoire said, "Is not Persian, but is okay."

Romeo loved the armoire. It added elegance to his bedroom, much in the same way the Persian rug his cousin had given him added class to his living room. There wasn't a great deal of either in a Public Defender's apartment.

He had jumped out the shower and stood in basketball shorts, still dripping water on the floor in front of his grand armoire. He stared at his reflection in the full-length mirror inside the left door and thought of Chelsea.

She had been on his mind ever since he'd run into her in the parking lot that day. Even with her baby bump, he was reminded of the young, innocent girl whose mother had forced her upon him.

There was also the phone call he had received that afternoon.

The day before, he had gotten a visit from an old client, Marcus "Black" Nelson. Black was just a small-time hooligan, but he worked for his older brother, Mario "Rio" Nelson, who had been a heavy player in Detroit's underworld. Romeo had represented Black a half-dozen times or so, usually getting him off with only a fine or probation. Romeo was surprised to see him standing outside his office wearing a crispy white T-shirt and heavy gold chain. Usually, their interactions began with a jailhouse collect call and one of them wearing county orange.

"Yo, Mr. Q.!" He extended his hand. "I was wondering if you had a minute."

"What'd you do, Marcus?" Romeo said, using his arm to usher Black into his office.

Black walked into Romeo's modest office. There was just a desk, a plain oak bookcase, and two leather chairs. Black sat down in one of them.

"Nothing. But they arrested me yesterday. Talkin' about me and my cousin held up this liquor store. Then a couple of hours later they let me go, because I was at the casino all day, on camera!" he snarled.

Between Black's past crimes and his present affiliations, this wasn't the first time the police had targeted him as a person of interest.

"We both know what it is. But it don't matter. My probation officer is trying to violate me now. I'm not supposed to have no police contact. They setting me up trying to get me to snitch on my brother. I need your help," he pleaded.

Romeo accepted payment in kind. And for some of his clients, that meant favors, the kind he may have preferred to keep on the low. Sometimes in the pursuit of justice, he found it necessary to use less than scrupulous methods to acquire information.

"Can you make this go away?" Black had pulled a large wad of cash out of his pocket and dropped it on the table.

"The state pays me. I don't need that," Romeo replied as he always did to Black when he tried to throw his brother's dirty money around.

"I know the more money, the harder a mouthpiece gon' work. I need you to be motivated." The young man was bold and arrogant.

"Why don't you take your money and retain one of those tailored suits over at Feinstein, Bristoll and Lewis?"

"C'mon, Mr. Q. You the best lawyer I ever had. Even if you is free."

Romeo was typing Marcus's name into his client database to confirm that his probation officer was still Stephanie Holmes. He had just seen her at a cocktail party hosted by the Detroit Institute of Arts. She was flirtatious. He could talk her out of writing up the violation.

"You want to motivate me? I'll tell you what I need from you," he said.

"Anything," Black said eagerly, leaning forward.

"Information," Romeo said plainly.

"What kind of information?"

"I need you to find out what, if anything, the Fontaines are planning to do to the man that killed Boudreaux."

Black's eyes got big. He leaned back in the chair and exhaled.

"I need a real good reason to be on Joy Road. We are Puritan Avenue. And the PA boys don't like to go south of Schoolcraft. Everybody know that," he said righteously.

"Well, the County Prosecutor Kim Worthy, wants you to snitch on your brother and all your PA friends. It's either do this for me, or do that for her, or...?" Romeo dangled a third option.

"Or what?" Black asked.

"Take the five years, probably get out in three. You were at the casino yesterday, but we're not going to pretend that you don't violate your parole everyday. Seen your brother lately?" Romeo answered calmly.

Black smacked his lips. "Why do you care what they do? You a A-rab in a downtown office. You ain't even on the block!"

Romeo didn't have the patience to explain to Black again that people from Iran were not Arabs. Even though it was his biggest pet peeve. Instead, he gave him an answer.

"I have a friend that is close to that man. I need to know if she's safe or not. She's carrying his baby. You do this for me, and I'll get Ms. Holmes to forgive you this time," Romeo said.

Black stared back at him while he considered his options. "I'll put my ear to the streets and see what I can find out for you. Now call her."

The next afternoon, Romeo had taken Stephanie Holmes to lunch. She tried several times to grab him by the manhood under the table and licked his ear in the parking lot before agreeing to drop the violation. Later, he received a call from Black. It was brief.

"Get your girl somewhere safe. I didn't get details, but it's something about the baby. You didn't hear this from me."

He hung up.

A few hours later, Romeo stood in front of his cherrywood armoire staring at his wet body, consumed with thoughts of Chelsea and how he could protect her. He knew he had to tell Carter. He had only initiated the inquiry in hopes of putting Carter's mind at ease. But how would he tell his best friend that gangsters were gunning for his sister's unborn baby? In Detroit, a death wish almost always led to a death.

He sat on his bed and grabbed his phone off the nightstand. He needed to talk to her. But he couldn't just call her. It had been too long. What would she think of him coming out of the blue? What if the stress caused harm to the baby? And yet, five years later, after only one night together, he felt an intense need to protect her.

If he was being honest, ever since he and Carter had gone to the game, he had wanted to talk to her. He wanted to hear every detail of the murders she had solved. Why couldn't she be brilliant when he had needed her to be? How did she end up dating a man that could kill another man? Why would she choose single parenting over success with him? Obviously, when he had run into her, he couldn't talk like he wanted to, but seeing her and touching her had brought back a feeling. Not even a feeling. Maybe just a thought.

Totty bounced out of the bathroom wearing two of Romeo's towels. One around her body and one around her head.

"Want to go to Sweetwater? I could go for some wings and a beer. Why are you still so wet?" She glanced down at the puddle on the floor. She removed her body towel and tossed it to him. He looked up at her naked body.

"You are so beautiful, Totty."

She smiled at him. "Thanks, Babe."

"I don't think we should see each other anymore." He stood and returned to his armoire.

Totty's smile faded and turned into surprise. She stood motionless and watched as he quickly dressed.

"I had a long day, and maybe it's put me in a mood, but," he paused, "meedoonam hanooz ba doost dokhtare ghableet hastee. I don't want to make a big deal. Ok? It is what it is."

She stared quietly. But he could see the storm brewing behind her confusion.

"I have to go. I have an emergency. Do me a favor, lock the door on your way out." He stuffed a wallet and phone into his pockets and exited the room. He grabbed his car keys from off a hook by the front door and closed it, hearing the siren screeching of Totty's cursing at him in the background.

He was also tired of her calling him an Arab.

Chapter Thirty-nine

Snap was semi-drunk in Chuck's Millionaire's Club, looking at what he considered to be a lack of effort on the part of the women in the room.

"Yoga pants and flip-flops. Bad weaves and fake ponytails. These broads ain't even trying!" he said with an air of disgust.

"If she wearin' yoga pants, it's because she wants you to see what she working with," Darius chimed in from the left of him, three drinks past semi-drunk.

"Yeah. You see a lack of effort. I see easy to undress," Ron harmonized from the right.

Darius and Ron had been friends with Snap for years. Not close friends, but hound dog friends. They were all regulars at Chuck's, and Darius only called when he wanted to invite Snap to somewhere women would be. He liked to hunt the ladies as a pack. Ron was normally the more rational between the two, until the liquor took hold of his good senses and then he became equally as salacious.

"I shoulda stayed home. I'm just spending money for nothing. Ain't no bad chicks in here tonight, and I could get drunk with yaw anytime, for less money," Snap said.

"Shut up!" Ron said adamantly. "You just want to rush back home so you can sit up under Chelsea like you always do."

"Chels went to Phoenix," Snap lied.

"She crazy. Always walking somewhere. If my Pops had an ol' lady that hit the number, you can best believe I'd be taking a limo everywhere I go," Ron said finishing another drink.

"Chelsea ain't crazy."

Darius shot Ron a glare. The kind that reminded Ron how Snap always defended Chelsea.

"I'm mad at her for getting pregnant by a dude like James. He ain't all that. Loser job, no bread and he wasn't even treating her right. Now she just another thot on the block with a baby by a brother in jail," Darius said.

Snap perked up. Darius had caught his attention.

"What do you mean, 'he wasn't treating her right'? He wasn't hitting her or nothing like that."

There were about ten seconds of awkward silence while Ron and Darius exchanged eye-dancing glances. It was as if they were having an entire conversation in their heads.

"Don't look at him! Answer me! What did you mean by that?" Snap said, standing up and facing both of his friends so that he could see their faces together.

"Well," Ron said, "Dude was in here all the time with other chicks."

Snap gave a hard exhale. "He was cheating on her?"

"All the time," Darius said. "We thought you knew. I mean, we knew she didn't know. But as much as you be in here, how did you not see it?"

Snap shrugged his shoulders. "He must didn't want me to see him."

"I know he got paid on Thursdays, 'cause that was the day he'd usually come in here with some ho, showing off and spending money," Ron added.

A few months back, before James was arrested, Snap was spending most of his Thursday evenings watching football. He was in Carter's fantasy league, and the two had a side bet on practically every game. He remembered how annoyed Chelsea was to be left alone every week because she thought James was working late on Thursdays.

"Whatever," he said. "She's better off without him."

"Maybe you can put the good word in for me," Darius said to Snap with a devilish grin.

"Maybe you should see how her body look after she have that baby," Ron countered.

"Yaw dumb!" Snap laughed out loud. He beckoned the waitress for another round that would put him on the other side of semi-drunk.

An hour later, he was standing seriously close to one of the yoga pants girls urging her to give him her phone number. And it hit him like a fast car.

Bou Fontaine was killed on a Thursday night.

"Wait a minute, Baby, I gotta be Watson again," he said, dismissing the girl as he walked away. He scanned the room for Ron and Darius. He had a very important question to ask.

He finally saw them in the corner of the bar across the room. Darius was locking lips with a woman against the wall and Ron was seated with a woman on his lap. Snap, trying to shake off the blur, made his way over to them and sat next to Ron.

"Hey! Was James here the night that Bou Fontaine got killed?" he asked directly.

The girl on Ron's lap got up and quickly walked away.

"Man! What's wrong with you?" Ron asked, irritated.

"Answer my question, Dog!"

Darius had stopped kissing that other woman and was now staring down at Ron and Snap. For the second time in one night, it was obvious they were keeping a secret. Snap lowered his eyes and tightened his lips. Ron nodded slowly.

"So yaw knew and didn't say nothing? He's in jail!" Snap said loudly. Fortunately, the music drowned him out.

"Look, Man, I ain't seent a thang! I don't need the Fontaines kicking in my door," Ron said honestly.

Snap got up and walked outside. It was time to do what he should have done when Luc threatened Chelsea. Call Carter.

Carter answered the phone, "What up Snap?"

Snap could hear music in the background. He wasn't the only person out having a drink. "Where you at, Bro?"

"The Mixx. You good?"

"I need to talk to you, Car. It's really important. I'm at Chuck's. Have a drink with me. Or, I guess I can come over there. Don't matter."

"Yo. You sound funny. What's wrong?" Carter replied.

The sounds of the bar had died down. Carter must have stepped into a quiet space.

"I'll tell you when I see you."

"Well, I'll come to Chuck's. I need an excuse to leave here anyway. My partner has been talking my head off about her love problems. Let me settle up here. Be there in a few."

Chapter Forty

Romeo had left his flat and headed straight for the freeway. He was an eastsider, and Carter lived in the northwest suburbs. It would take a good forty-five minutes to get across town. He stopped and got some gas on Jefferson Avenue en route to I-75. It was a popular gas station because it was the only one in the heart of downtown. So, sometimes customers had to wait in line to get to a pump. The end of summer had brought out the motorcyclists who either all needed gas at the same time or just congregated in the parking lot to make it difficult for cars to get through. It took Romeo fifteen minutes to fill his tank for the long ride out to Novi Township.

He didn't want to talk to Carter over the phone, but thought it best to call ahead. When he got back in the car after, he picked his phone up off the passenger seat and saw that Totty had called him fourteen times.

He turned off the phone and didn't turn it back on until he pulled up in front of Carter's condo. All the lights were off. If he wasn't at home, he was either working, shopping, or drinking and chasing women.

Carter was not working. If they were on a case, Totty would have said so. No one bragged about how hard she worked more than Totty. The stores were closed, so Carter must have been at that dingy old bar all the cops went to after work.

He had nineteen voice messages, all from Totty. He decided to try calling Carter again.

Carter answered and he could hear music in the background. But before he even had a chance to say hello, Carter said, "Bro! I was just trying to hook you up. I'm not a couples' counselor!"

"You're with Totty?" he asked, rolling his eyes.

"Yeah. She just bum rushed me at The Mixx. Man! What did you do?" Carter asked, still laughing.

Romeo took a breath before speaking. Just because he had prioritized talking to Carter didn't mean that he didn't have any legitimate grievances with Totty. And why was he automatically assumed to be the bad guy?

"I can't come up there. Let's go somewhere else," Romeo said invoking the "bros before hoes" clause of any male friendship.

"Alright. Snap just called me. I told him I'd meet him up at Chuck's on Plymouth. You know where that is?" Carter said.

"Yeah. Give me about half an hour. I'm at your house."

"Why didn't you call me before you drove out there?"

"Ask Totty," Romeo said before hanging up the phone.

At least she had stopped calling him. But when Carter left her, she might start back up. Romeo turned off the phone again, just in case. One crisis at a time.

He changed the radio station until he heard some mellow, slow grooves. He usually listened to talk radio, political debates and the like. But for the next thirty minutes, he just wanted to hear some sad love songs from the '90s.

Chapter Forty-one

Carter got into his convertible Audi, made an illegal U-turn on Livernois Avenue and headed south toward I-96. Livernois was a six-lane street. At this time of night with the residents of University District tucked safely in their beds, it was an empty six-lanes. It was the perfect time to put the pedal to the medal and open up all eight cylinders. One of the perks of the job.

He had barely finished one beer when Totty had brought full hysteria into the bar. She was talking so fast Carter was hardly able to keep up. Ro had been acting weird, barely talking. She said they made love, took a shower and he dumped her while she was naked. Of course, being Romeo's friend she expected Carter to disclose the secrets behind the actions. But he couldn't because he didn't know. He had tried to explain to her that Romeo wasn't the type of guy to call whining about any woman. Not his style. That morsel of truth didn't make Totty feel any better. In fact, it made her scream out, "Why would he need to whine about me?"

Not ten minutes later, Snap had called him up with his serious voice. Snap was never serious. So Carter conjectured that he needed to borrow some money. He was happy for a reason to get out of the middle of Romeo and Totty.

And then, low and behold, Romeo calls. Now he probably wanted to tell Carter his side. It was going to be a long night. He paid his tab, and after saying goodbye to his friends, made an excuse, and left a distraught Totty sitting at the bar. He passed Woo at the door as he was leaving out. At least she wouldn't be alone.

If he was going to loan money and listen to love problems, at least he would speed down the street with the wind in his face, turning a fifteen-minute drive into an eight-minute one. He deserved the indulgence for being such a good friend. Carter whipped into the lot and parked next to the familiar black Escalade. He was usually paranoid about door dings, but he didn't have to worry about Snap hitting his car. The two men were equally fanatical about preserving their vehicles.

No sooner had Carter had exited the car than Romeo pulled his white Volvo into the very next spot. He wasn't driving his old Lincoln anymore. His mother finally decided that a lawyer needed a better car. So she purchased the Volvo she was leasing and gave it to Romeo. It was the perfect car for him. It was old enough that he could drive it and still feel like a man of the people. And the old Lincoln couldn't have made it from Novi back to the city that fast.

Carter and Romeo walked in together. Flashing the badge got the men around the security frisking that was common in neighborhood bars.

Snap was sitting at a hightop table in a corner of the room. He stood when he saw Car and Ro come in.

"What up, Ro Q? It's been a minute since I seen you." Snap extended a dap and a half-hug to Romeo.

"Sup, Snap. What's good?" Ro responded.

"Nothing much. What up, Car?" Snap repeated the greeting and the gesture.

The three men sat, and Carter immediately began looking for a waitress. "Yaw both look way too serious. I need a drink."

"I found out tonight that James was cheating on Chels. Bringing women here," Snap blurted out.

"What? Man, I'm beating his ass when he gets out of jail," Carter said, half-joking.

"I have a client in Dickerson who'll beat his ass right now if you want," Romeo quipped. He and Carter laughed. Snap wasn't laughing. "Car, he used to come in with a broad every Thursday, when Chelsea thought he was at work. Every Thursday."

Carter's face sobered. "How do you know?"

Snap pointed in the direction of two inebriated men slouching over a table. "They told me."

"Why didn't they tell us?" Carter stood up to talk to them. Snap pulled him back onto his bar stool.

"They are totally wasted. Besides, the Fontaines are scarier than you. But you have to admit, this changes everything."

"What's going on?" Romeo asked.

"Bou was murdered on a Thursday. James was the best suspect because he didn't have an alibi," Carter shared.

"You need to get that information to the Fontaines asap. They're looking for revenge. This lets Chels off the hook," Romeo stated firmly.

"It does. She asked me not to tell you, but Luc low-key threatened her last week. That's why she went to Boca," Snap said.

"Luc? He threatened my sister?" Carter stood up. "What exactly did he say?"

"He told her to take care of her baby."

"I'm going to find him!" Carter tried to storm out, but Romeo grabbed him.

"No, Car. Let's get all the facts straight."

Romeo was always the voice of reason. He wasn't weak, he was calculating. And he thought like a lawyer. He wouldn't want Carter to do anything that might get him in trouble. Carter trusted him.

"Alright. What do we know?" Carter asked.

Romeo heaved a deep sigh and told Carter what he had heard from Black. Carter dropped his head into his hands and leaned forward on the table. Romeo put his hand on Carter's shoulder.

Snap's eyes had the glassy look of a man holding back tears. "Yo, this ain't happening. We can't let this happen. I don't care about James. But nobody hurts Chelsea or the baby. They gotta find another way."

Carter jumped in. "They don't want a war with the police."
"Wait," Romeo intervened again, "if James has an alibi., why can't you just reopen the investigation? That should calm the Fontaines until you find the real killer."

"James is guilty. The word of two drunken barflies won't convince me otherwise. It definitely won't convince Arcangelo Fontaine."

"It raises doubts for me," Romeo said.

"That's because you're thinking like a defense attorney. I'm trying to protect my family!" Carter was trying hard to compose his emotions.

"Maybe to protect your family, you need a defense attorney. Proving James is not the killer might be your only hope."

"Ro is right. Chelsea said he wasn't guilty all along. He has an alibi now. We need to convince the Fontaines," Snap said.

"I'm a police officer. I can't just hand them someone else to harm in her place. They need to be put away."

"I'm not saying trade the baby for another child. I'm saying, use the facts to buy some time. The only way out of this is to dig deep into it." Romeo had a way of giving arguments even when there was no trial.

Carter offered a slow nod. He understood what Snap and Romeo were saying, but it just was not the way police officers did things. They put potential victims in safe houses, pursued violent criminals. They didn't reopen murder cases and admit they made a mistake.

But maybe the police way wasn't going to work for his sister. "We need to make a plan. Let's get some whiskey." Romeo waved and caught the attention of the waitress, who smiled when she saw him.

When she brought the first round of whiskeys to the table, she leaned in and said to Romeo, "It's on me, Handsome."

Carter and Snap snickered like teenage boys.

"He's beefing with Totty as we speak, and still he charms waitresses!"

Romeo laughed. "I'm not beefing with Totty. All things considered, I think I was kind to her. Now my Uncle Babak would've handled her differently."

"Am I hearing this right? The Hottie?" Snap asked.

"Ro was seeing Totty. And then today, he dumped her. I know this because she spent an hour telling me how horribly he treated her." Carter laughed. "I know he's the 'love them and leave them' type because he dumped my sister too!"

Romeo spit his whiskey out in laughter. "That's cold! You can't compare Chelsea to Totty!"

"You got a pattern, Dude!" Carter said, still laughing.

"Totty was still seeing Woo. She thought I didn't know. I got tired of her lying to me," he said plainly.

Carter and Snap stopped laughing.

Carter thought that she was done with Woo when he invited her to meet Romeo at the baseball game. Uh-oh.

"I don't know why she's playing the victim. I told her what it was before I left."

"You said you didn't want to make a big deal out of it." Totty had told him that much.

"I don't. It is what it is. But I said it to her face, 'Look, I know you're still seeing your ex' and... wait a minute," Romeo's voice trailed as he got lost in thought. "I might not have said that part in English."

The men howled with laughter. Carter had seen Romeo slip in and out of Farsi when he was upset. It was hilarious.

Carter appreciated the distraction of Romeo's ever-chaotic love life. But no matter how much he laughed now, he would have to face this Fontaine situation head-on. Protecting Chelsea was his duty.

Telling her was his new dread. She couldn't know about James and the other women until after she had the baby. He wouldn't be responsible for adding any stress in those final weeks. So like a good big brother, he would carry it all for her. But make no mistake, no one would harm his sister or his nephew.

Carter would do whatever was necessary.

Chapter Forty-two

"So, how's it going?" Carter said as soon as Chelsea answered the phone.

"Not as terrible as it could be," Chelsea said.

"What have you been up to?"

"Bored. But Poochie told me that I'm supposed to be bored when I'm pregnant. I was never bored in Detroit."

"That's because you had me. Now you just got Maddy and Dad. Do I even want to ask how many episodes of Criminal Minds they made you watch?"

"A million. What's up with you?"

"Me and Snap painted the baby's room. We're doing the living room this weekend."

"Thank you," Chelsea said, but she didn't mean it. Even though he had every right, it still irritated her when Carter just let himself into her house.

"It's blue, in case you were wondering," he teased.

"I don't care. And I doubt Babe will either. What else is good?" Chelsea was desperate for news from home. Anything had to be better than another Criminal Minds marathon.

"I know about Luc," he said calmly. Not at all the reaction she was expecting from him.

"Snap told you. Don't do anything crazy. I've had some time to think about it and maybe I was overreacting." The Fontaines had always been dramatic with the Hatian accents and the flamboyant, colorful jackets. "Luc just surprised me."

Carter was quiet long enough for Chelsea to notice. When he finally spoke, his words were slow and deliberate.

"Some information has come to light," he began.

As he caught her up on Romeo's intel, she gasped and forgot to start breathing again.

"Chelsea! Breathe!" Carter yelled into the phone. She had a 25-year habit of stress-related apnea. "I'm going to protect you."

"Maybe I should go to Arizona and stay with Uncle Aaron. I don't want Daddy involved in any of this."

Diane's younger brother, Aaron, had once been a drug dealer when he lived in Detroit twenty years ago. He got arrested and was released on a technicality. The brush with a life sentence was the wake-up call he needed. He took the money he had stashed and bought a house in Arizona. He's been running a successful landscaping business ever since. He was now a blend of street and respectability. It was a perfect hiding spot.

"You're in a gated community with 24-hour security. It's the best place you could be. Besides, you're not due for six more weeks. So we have time to fix this," Carter said.

"Fix the Fontaines?"

"Narcotics is building a case against them, we'll have leverage. We can make this go away if we have enough time. Just need you to sit tight for a while."

Chelsea heaved a frustrated sigh. At least she had started breathing again. "I don't want to stay here."

"Well, too bad your rap friend can't take you to Barcelona. But you don't have a passport. So you're stuck in Boca."

"What am I supposed to do here for the next six weeks, Carter?"

"I don't know. Maybe somebody will get murdered. In the meantime, drink your milk and put your feet up."

Chelsea knew Carter as well as she knew herself. She didn't have to tilt her head or scrunch her face to know when he was lying or withholding something. But he was her big brother, and she trusted him with her life. So if he said to sit tight, she would maybe try to oblige him.

"Maybe somebody will get murdered," she said, mocking Carter. Somebody did. That's what started all this drama.

Even if she was tightly sitting, she still wanted to know what he wasn't telling her. She could ask Romeo, but calling him would be weird. It would be much easier to trick the information out of Snap. Chelsea considered it a lie of necessity.

Chapter Forty-three

"How's my Boo?" Snap answered the phone playfully.

"Car told me to sit tight while he fixes the Fontaines," she replied.

"It's for the best, Chels, we have to keep you and Babe safe. It shouldn't be too long before it's all worked out."
"He told me everything, Snap. Everything."

"Just because James was with another girl doesn't mean he was having sex."

Snap and Carter had debated whether or not to tell Chelsea about the other woman, women... before eventually agreeing it was best for the sake of the baby to keep her calm. So Carter would leave out certain details about the Fontaine hit and not one word about James's cheating. Snap had wondered why he told her.

"What other girl? When?" Chelsea screamed into the phone.

Or had Chelsea just tricked him into giving it up. "You just said..." his voice trailed.

"Devin Haines, you better tell me about this other girl or I'm never speaking to you again!"

Poor Snap. This wasn't the first time he had found his loyalty being tested by the French children. He usually sided with Chelsea, but Carter had made a good point about keeping her from getting too upset. She was pregnant. And she did have a bad temper. But since she was clearly upset anyway, now the safest thing to do was to tell her.

So he did.

She hung up the phone on him.

At 4:30 am the following morning she had called him back.

"I'm at the airport. Come get me."

"Yup. Text me the gate," he said groggily.

He wasn't surprised that she had flown back. He halfway expected it.

Thirty-five minutes later he pulled up at the Delta terminal. She was easy to spot. In just three weeks her strut had degraded to a full blown waddle. She was struggling with her luggage.

Snap jumped out the Escalade and jogged toward her.

"Slow down, Preggers. You doin' too much." He took the bags from her and hoisted them into the back of his SUV. "I don't remember you leaving with so many bags."

"I had a shower. I got some nice stuff." She stared at the open passenger door. After Snap closed the hatchback he walked around and lifted Chelsea into the car.

"Thank you. I don't think I can do SUVs anymore, too much climbing."

Snap had been awake less than forty-five minutes after three hours of sleep and a sixteen-hour shift. He was tired. But the obvious questions couldn't be avoided.

"What's the move, Chels?" he asked, speeding back to the freeway.

"We have to go to Dickerson and find out why the lying dummy didn't tell the police he had an alibi!"

"Yo! Are you serious? Are you saying what I think you are?" Snap didn't know whether to be excited or worried.

"This whole time I've been saying that James didn't kill Bou. But it was just instinct. I know my man. He ain't a killer. But I learned something from watching Criminal Minds. It's all about the evidence. Carter had it. I didn't. It's real easy to catch a lie when somebody's lying."

"But all we knew about Bou's murder was what Carter told us," Snap added.

"Right," she said, chewing on some Tums that she had pulled out of her purse. "I wouldn't have been able to figure out who killed Steven Harris if I hadn't seen his office."

"The Case of the Body in the Closet!"

"And I only knew to check Picture Me Clubbin' because I saw the pictures in Kevin's house."

"The Case of the Shady Boyfriend!" Snap cheered.

"I wouldn't have figured out how Lee Bee got robbed if I hadn't noticed the trash."

Snap was all smiles. "The Case of The Diamond Mic."

Chelsea chuckled. "Stop trippin'. I'm trying to get to a point."

"Carter said putting the Fontaines in jail is the only way."

"Well," Chelsea said, "that's why I called you for a ride and not him."

"I thought it was because I live closer to the airport."

"True. It would've taken him an hour to get out of the house."

"He has to iron his airport outfit."

Chelsea and Snap laughed. She ate more Tums. And then forced him to stop at Coney Island for breakfast.

Chapter Forty-four

Chelsea hadn't thought about sleep once she arrived home. First she ate, then she unpacked all of her baby's new knickknacks, inspected the paint job in the nursery, and went online to order shelves. When she finally had laid down, it was almost 8 AM. She couldn't go to sleep because of her constant heartburn. It took her about an hour to drift off. But she was too anxious to stay asleep.

By 11:30, she was up and dressed. Visiting Dickerson was her priority. But the thought of climbing into Snap's large vehicle vexxed her.

She put a fresh pack of Tums in her purse, grabbed her keys and opened her back door. She tapped the garage door remote before locking the door. Ray French had the remote installed shortly after delivery of her guilt car.

After the money came, Maddy wanted to provide for her children. She had begun the task of finding new homes for each of her three. Ray French had to remind her that Carter was also her child now, and Chelsea. As co-workers, Maddy and Chelsea had gotten along well enough. Chelsea was Mr. Ali's favorite because she executed her duties flawlessly, and as manager Maddy also appreciated her good work. But as stepmother and stepdaughter, their relationship had deteriorated to a dismal point. It was with great reluctance that, when purchasing luxury vehicles for her children, she included Chelsea. She knew this because Maddy had told her as much.

One day, without Chelsea's knowledge, Ray had driven off in the 2007 Dodge Caliber and returned in the black 2007 Mustang Shelby. It was the very first GT 500 King of The Road off the assembly line. Ray had purchased the car at a tax auction.

The original owner was a Ford Motor Company Board Member. The second owner had acquired it privately for $689,000. The IRS had seized it, but not before enhancements were made to the electrical and audio systems. Despite the car's rich pedigree, Chelsea, who knew nothing about automobiles, took umbrage with the fact that everyone else got new cars and hers was used. Ray French said, "Wait until you hear the motor. It could hum perfect harmony with the Mighty Temptations."

The garage door opened on the polycotton car cover. Chelsea shuffled into the garage and pulled it off. She fell into the driver's side, which was much easier than ascending that high step on Snap's Escalade. One more of those and she was going to end up giving birth in his front seat.

Snap had driven the car while she was out of town so she had to do a little wrangling to adjust the seat back to a short person's comfort. She started the car. Ray was right. The engine hummed, maybe not Temptations, but at least Boys II Men. She slowly pulled her car out of the garage, reversed down the driveway, then stopped just short of the curb. She took out her phone to send Snap a text message. *You ready? I'm outside.*

His response was quick. *Did you call Uber? I can drive.*

Just come on.

She had sworn that she would never drive the car...but she had a baby to protect. And love was stronger than pride. She had to find out who killed Bou. The only lead was the fact that James had not been honest about his alibi. She needed to know what he was hiding. Then a conversation with Luc, if only to buy time to find the real killer. It was that simple.

A few minutes later Snap came outside.

"Yooooooo!" he said running down the stairs. He sprawled his body across the windshield and looked Chelsea in the face. "What is going on?"

Chelsea laughed, and Snap joined her inside the car.

"I told you I couldn't do the SUV anymore."

"Chels! You're driving!"

"I know, I know. But I can't find a killer in the back of an Uber."

Snap sighed. "Are you sure you want to do this, Chels?"

"Yes. I had a dream on the plane. I was in a house with S. Epatha Merkerson and Shemar Moore. She kept saying, 'You are a cashier, a Black woman, a mom,' and he kept saying, 'Babygirl, he's protecting somebody.' So I woke up and wondered, was it me? Or was it the real killer? Either way, I gotta talk to the boyfriend."

"I think you need some sleep."

"Nope. My mind is clear," she said while the car sailed toward the freeway. It drove like a dream. "You've been the one telling me to be a detective."

"I did, but..." he started.

"It's the only way. Are you in, Devin?"

"You ain't doing this without me."

"Good. I don't want to."

"You sure you can handle this car? Maybe I should drive."

Chelsea answered him by pushing her foot on the gas pedal. "Listen to that engine humming like Dru Hill."

"What?"

"Never mind, I said it wrong."

The Dickerson Correctional Facility was not lined with fencing and armed guards sitting high up in towers the way Chelsea had expected. To the contrary, it was lined with trees and an inviting driveway that opened up into a parking lot not too different from the average American shopping center. Chelsea was just about fed up with Snap's criticisms of her driving when she made her final turn into the facility. She had never been to any jail before.

Snap advised Chelsea not to park the Shelby next to another car. "We don't want her getting door dings. What are you going to call her?"

"Maddy bought it. So, Side Piece?"

Snap laughed, "No, Chels, it has to be an old lady name, like Lerlene or Barbara."

"How about Diane?" she asked as she pulled into her parking space that was exactly four spots away from the next nearest car.

"Perfect." Snap had unfastened his seatbelt and opened the passenger door. "Oh yeah, you can't take anything inside. Not even a phone. Just put your ID in your pocket."

She pulled her driver's license out of her purse and tussled out of the car.

"Chelsea! What are you doing here?" Carter was yelling out of the window of his Audi as he pulled into the adjacent parking space.

Chelsea threw her eyebrows up. Carter wouldn't believe a recurring Law and Order dream had made her break her promise to stay in Florida. "I thought we had a plan! Snap told you about some hoes, and you got on a plane? Dad is pissed!" he yelled as he approached her.

Snap stepped in between the siblings. Pregnancy wouldn't stop Chelsea from pushing her big brother.

"Why didn't you tell me about the hoes?" she yelled back at him. "And be careful! You better not ding Diane!"

"Why are you driving? And why is your car Diane? How do you know my car ain't Diane?"

"I just assumed your car was Madeleine!"

Carter pushed Snap aside, grabbed Chelsea by the forearm and tried to force her back into the car.

"You're going back to the airport!" he insisted.

"I'm gon' find out who killed Bou like you shoulda did!" she said, snatching away from him.

"Chelsea! Carter! This is a prison!" Romeo's voice bellowed out the window across the two cars as he pulled his Volvo into the spot next to Carter's car. "You will both be banned, and no one will be allowed to speak with James!"

"Man! What are you doing here?" Carter asked before Chelsea could get the words out.

Romeo took his time rolling up his car window and shutting off his vehicle. He reached across the back seat and pulled an Attache case off the floor. He opened his car door, swung his legs out and brushed the lint off of his pants before he stood up. "I could ask you the same question."

"I'm going inside to talk to James," Chelsea said. "With or without you, Carter!"

"No, I'm going in without you," he replied.

"He didn't talk to you before. Why would he now?" she asked smugly.

"Chelsea's right," Romeo interjected. "She has the best chance of getting him to open up."

Carter agreed to let Chelsea go into the prison, but only if Romeo went with her. He was a defense attorney. He knew the facility well.

"You expect me to go with my old boyfriend? What is this? Love and Hip Hop?" She was angry with James, but she wasn't trying to torture him. Seeing her with a man like Romeo would make him crazy. He was looking exceptionally fetching in his brown suit.

So Carter agreed to allow Snap to go inside, but only if Chelsea let him go for a spin in her Mustang.

"This is a bad idea," Carter said, unlocking the Mustang doors.

"She got this," Romeo reassured. "I think this case needs a new set of eyes. And Chelsea has beautiful eyes."

Carter stared at Romeo in bewilderment before he got into the car. The two men zoomed out of the driveway just as Snap and Chelsea reached the giant steel door that separated the prison from the nice parking lot. She hesitated.

"Scared?" He asked her.

"Point of no return."

"So, what do you want to do?"

"Let's go talk to a cheater about a murder."

Can Chelsea prove James didn't kill Bou Fontaine before the Fontaines put their plan of revenge in motion? Can she do it before she gives birth?

Find out in the next exciting Shorty Book:
Mama's Baby,
Daddy's Murder.

Made in the USA
Columbia, SC
16 July 2022